SPIRIT
NIGHTS

SPIRIT NIGHTS

NIGHTS

EASTERINE KIRE

BARB
ICAN
PRESS

Published by Barbican Press: London & Los Angeles

Copyright © Easterine Kire, 2022

Registered office: 1 Ashenden Road, London E5 0DP

www.barbicanpress.com

@barbicanpress1

Cover by Rawshock Design

Cover photograph by Seyie Suohu

With thanks to Tromsø Library for their kind support of this publication

A CIP catalogue for this book is available from the British Library

ISBN: 978-1-909954-54-0

Typeset in Bembo

Typeset by Imprint Digital Ltd

Printed and bound by CPI Group (UK) Ltd, Croydon CR0 4YY

About Easterine Kire

Dr Easterine Kire is a poet, short story writer and novelist, born in Kohima, Nagaland, Northeast India. She writes from 'the frontline of contemporary indigenous literature'.

Nagaland stretches either side of the border between Myanmar and Indian State of Assam. This is ancient tribal hill country, and Kire writes from inside the fiercely independent Naga culture.

In 1982, she was the first Naga poet in English to have her poetry published. In 2003, she wrote *A Naga Village Remembered,* the first Naga novel in English. Kire has also been the first Naga writer to write books for children.

In 2011 she was awarded the Governor's medal for excellence in Naga literature. Her novel, *Bitter Wormwood* was shortlisted for the Hindu Lit for Life prize in 2013. In the same year she received the Veu LLiure Prize (Free Voice Prize) from Pen Català.

The City of Tromsø, and Norwegian PEN invited Easterine Kire to Tromsø, inside Norway's Arctic Circle, where she has lived since 2005. She is a member of the Norway-based band, Jazzpoesi, and a founder member of Barkweaver publications which gathers folk tales and people stories. In 2013 Jazzpoesi released a digital CD in 2013 which topped the Norwegian jazz charts.

In 2015, her novel, *When the River Sleeps* was awarded The Hindu Literature prize. *Son of the Thundercloud* won both the Bal Sahitya Puraskar of the Sahitya Academy and the 2017 Tata Literature Live Book of the Year award.

Kire holds a PhD in English Literature from Poona University. She performs poetry, delivers lectures on culture and literature, and holds writing workshops in schools and colleges.

Early appreciation of *Spirit Nights*

'To read Easterine Kire is to fall under the spell of an easeful, velvety, pitch-perfect storytelling. Spirit Nights brings together the lull of fable, the revelation of allegory, the vitality of folklore and the intimacy of the familial in a manner that is distinctly Kire. This book is especially memorable for a powerful female protagonist whose age-ripened wisdom is needed to save a community on the verge of being engulfed and erased by darkness.' – Gayathri Prabhu

'A rich festival of storytelling – playful, poignant and profound. Easterine Kire reimagines marvels for new audiences, shining fresh light on ancient wisdom and revealing truths that have united humanity for centuries. A beautiful read.' – Ann Morgan

And appreciation of Easterine Kire

'In an extraordinary fury of poems, short stories, histories, novels, and a separate profusion of words and music she calls jazzpoetry, this quietly irrepressible one-woman cultural renaissance has pioneered, nurtured, led and exemplified the modern literary culture of Nagaland, while also establishing herself in the front line of contemporary indigenous literature.' – Vivek Menezes, *Scroll*

'Easterine Kire is the keeper of her people's memory, their griot. She is a master of the unadorned language that moves because of the power of its evocative simplicity.' – Prof Emeritus Paul Pimomo

'Kire delicately mixes live traditions with new standards.' – Luis Gomez, *The National Herald*

Also by Easterine Kire:

Novels
Journey of the Stone
A Respectable Woman
Son of the Thundercloud
Don't Run My Love
When the River Sleeps
Bitter Wormwood
Life on Hold
Mari
A Terrible Matriarchy
A Naga Village Remembered

Short stories
The Rain Maiden and the Bear Man
Forest Song

Poetry
Jazzpoetry and other poems
A Slice of Stavanger
Ah, People of Tromsø
The Windhover Collection
Kelhoukevira

Non-Fiction
Walking the Roadless Road

Accounts of sudden darkness descending on the land exist in at least two tribal histories of the Naga people, the Rengma and the Chang. The story of Spirit Nights *is inspired by a story of darkness narrated by the Chang Naga tribe. Names and incidents are borrowed from the original tale. However, it must be clarified that it is not based on that story, but follows the path of fiction to achieve its telling.*

Prologue

The drumming could be heard all the way across the valley and well into the next. The men were beating the drum fast and furiously, a beat that any villager would recognise as a warning to return immediately to the village. They seemed to be competing with the darkness that was gathering just as swiftly; it was the great darkness that had descended in the middle of a sunny afternoon and made Namumolo's grandmother exclaim, '*Tiger has eaten the sun! Tiger has eaten the sun!*'

She began to shout loudly, '*Namu! Beat the drum! Get people back from the fields now!*' It was just too dangerous to be outside at this time. No one knew where the darkness had come from. Or why. One moment people were working their fields and tending to the paddy stalks that were beginning to bear grain, and in the next few moments, there was pandemonium as the sun suddenly disappeared and a perfectly clear sky turned dark and darker and darker still, until the darkness seemed to swallow the land. Even as they wasted precious minutes discussing if a storm was on the way and whether they should go home or wait it out, the sound of drums broke into their thoughts, each beat hurtling over the fields. The drumming was insistent and the beating desperate; everyone knew the rhythm that was being beaten. They were all taught to recognise it from childhood. The rapid, staccato bursts were only used to warn of great danger; the drums were calling out that there was not a second to waste. Every child of the village was taught this beat from childhood, so they all knew the immediacy of the danger it warned against. There was no time for arguments or questions.

'Hurry!' cried the older members to the younger. 'Leave that be! Leave everything behind and start running! Soto! Come out this instant. Is your hoe more precious than your life? Come on, we must go now. There is Death in those drums. We have to outrace him!'

The younger ones stopped dawdling and did as they were told. They saw their elders throwing their implements into the bushes, and they did the same and began to run, men carrying their children and women carrying their baskets. The darkness never let up. Some of the people stumbled on the narrow path from the fields to the village; others fell and cut themselves on wayside stones. But they quickly got up and kept on running, fear numbing their pain. There was no starlight to help them see the way in front of them because it was still afternoon – people were only halfway through their labours when the drums sounded. No one carried a wormwood torch, nor was there time to stop and make one. They had to get to the village as quickly as they could.

'Hunters!' shouted one of the elderly men. 'Lead us home!' As he called for hunters, four of the men ran forward and they led the way back, for they were the ones who knew their way about in the dark. Two young men came last, guarding those at the back and helping the weaker members.

Sweat broke out on Namu's brow and rolled downward as he pounded the giant drum with wooden pestles. The four men beating the log-drum were exhausted. They had been beating for more than an hour now, and the signals for warning against

danger were the most demanding. They beat the drum fren-
ziedly, punishingly, in their efforts to reach their villagers and
get them to safety. Their hands were beginning to ache from
the impact, but they could not stop. Not even to check if their
drumming had had any effect. The headman had told them that
on no account were they to stop drumming. They kept at it, not
exchanging a single word, grim-faced, each man buried deep in
his own thoughts. The darkness magnified sound. Each drum
beat travelled longer in the dark than it would by day; the sound
cut knife-like, through the gathering murkiness.

All the drummers had members of their families out in the
fields. They had stayed back in the village because it was their
turn to guard the village. And all this had happened on their
watch! They renewed their efforts at beating the big wooden
drum, as though that would hasten their people home.

'Tiger has eaten the sun!' Grandmother's words echoed in
Namu's ears. Whatever did Grandmother mean by that? As weird
as it sounded, Namu knew deep inside that his grandmother was
possibly the only person in their village who would know what
was happening.

Chapter One

'Grandmother! Look! I've caught three grasshoppers!'

The little boy ran excitedly to the old woman and held up his fist. She saw the crushed wings, legs and bruised green bodies of the insects he had caught.

'Can we eat them?' He was looking up eagerly at the grey-haired woman. The five-year-old had lost both his parents in a brutal enemy attack and his grandmother was the only parent he had ever known. He had only been a few months old when it happened. It was a wonder he had not been killed when their village was overrun and people were massacred in their own houses. Luckily for him, the killers had not seen the baby sleeping beside his mother and, having killed both adults in the house, the men escaped to avoid being caught in a counter attack.

'We don't eat grasshoppers, Namu. You can give that to our chickens and I will catch something else for you,' his grandmother replied. She broke off a broad leaf and handed it him. 'Here. Wrap them in this leaf and put it in your basket. We will take your catch home later.'

Tola, the old woman, worked hard to get enough food for the two of them. She had lost her husband ten years ago in a freak hunting accident. Namu's father had been her only son, and with him gone, Namu was the only family left to her. Tola tried to teach him the most important lesson of life, how to get food. They left early every morning to work at the *jhum* field where she had sowed hill rice. In the patches cleared for vegetables, she always had a good crop of chillies, tomatoes, egg plant, and beans growing. Native cabbages sprouted up in season, and if they plucked them before the caterpillars got to them, they made a nice addition to their evening meal. The tapioca and sweet potatoes grew wild and did well even though left quite untended. When they were out in the field, she would take her hoe and expertly dig out a few sweet potatoes for the boy. He loved to eat them raw, the juice dribbling down his chin. Namu was still too young to help, but he followed his grandmother around, carrying his little basket and imitating her as she plucked edible leaves and put them in her cane basket.

Tola checked the grain on the paddy stalks and satisfied herself that the ears were filling up. In three or four weeks they would turn yellow and be ready to be harvested. It was hard work, but it gave them food for a good part of the year. Like the rest of her fellow villagers, Tola owned a small terrace field down in the valley. Working in the field was a little less demanding than cultivating hill rice, and as she got older, the thought had crossed her mind that she should probably stop tilling the hill slopes altogether. Some years ago, she began to grow millet, which was also known by its native name, *the food of war*. It was so called because millet could be stocked for many months without spoiling, and when a village had been prevented by war from tilling their fields for months on end, they could still survive if they had millet in stock.

It was relatively easier to care for since the fast-growing millet plants required much less water than paddy. Weeding was done a few times during the growth season and the millet was always harvested before the rice. Those villagers who had big plots of land planted millet all along the edges. Tola had done as they did, sowing the hardy cereal after the second rain. As long as she was able to, she would provide food for them in the one way she knew, by tilling the ancestral fields that she and her husband owned. She had given up tilling her father's fields as it was too much work. Besides, they had enough food for the two of them. One day, Namu would inherit all the fields and plots of land owned by her and her husband. He would also inherit her father's lands because she was his only child, and the only other male relative who might have made claims on the land had more than sufficient land of his own.

Tola's hoe suddenly struck a rock, forcing her to stop digging. She instinctively put out her hand to check that the blade had not cracked from the impact. Then she looked at the sky; the sun was behind the plantain trees, wearing a halo of orange mist through which you could see the diaphanous wings of evening insects. It would linger there until it set, but on the days when Namu was with her, she preferred to set off for home earlier than the other field-goers.

'Come on, Namu, it's time to go home,' she called out to the boy. He had struggled halfway up a young Nutgall tree, trying to grab a bird's nest on the upper branches.

'But it's not dark yet, Grandmother,' Namu pleaded.

'And what are you going to do with the dark when it comes?' she asked in a rough voice. Namu knew that tone well. It brooked no arguments. He slung his basket on his back and followed her down the narrow path until it joined with the wider field path.

In the autumn months, Namu and his grandmother trapped small birds and locusts and dragonflies. Tola had a long stick with one end smeared with glue from mistletoe seeds, and she used it to trap unsuspecting dragonflies resting on paddy stalks. She taught Namu to smear leaves and branches with the glue and thoroughly cover the water surface in the stream with the smeared branches; at dawn, birds coming to drink water would get stuck on the leaves and wood. Early the next morning, the pair would run down to collect the birds they had trapped and they would take their catch home. Tola's job was to clean the birds and hang them over the fire to dry, while it fell to Namu to sweep the feathers into the fire and burn them. Tola cooked the meat with lightly pounded garlic and country ginger and red chilli. The broth was pungent and nourishing. In the winter months, she added three or four of the small, local tomatoes, after crushing them thoroughly so that the sourness would seep into the rest of the ingredients. The tomatoes gave the broth a tangy flavour that both of them liked.

As for the locusts and dragonflies, Tola always removed the wings and legs before roasting them lightly on the embers. She liked to sprinkle a little salt on top and serve the roasted meat atop warm rice. 'Eat, it's good for you,' she would tell Namu.

While the two were making their way home, Tola caught two green-backed frogs. As soon as they reached the house, she removed the entrails, chopped the meat and began to cook it in an old clay pot, adding fresh chilli, crushed garlic and tomatoes. Frog meat was considered medicinal in many tribes, and highly recommended for wounds and injuries, fevers and infections; people had such great faith in its healing properties. Boys were encouraged to catch them in the rainy season, and the surplus meat was dried over the hearth to be used sparingly. Frogs, river-crabs and snails were abundant in these months – seasonal food for the farmer.

The pungent aroma of crushed garlic wafted through the house.

'My mouth's watering, Grandmother. Are the frogs going to be tasty?'

'Oh yes,' she replied emphatically. 'Not only that, frog soup will give you strong legs like the frogs!'

When it was ready, she ladled out broth and rice in a bowl for him and the boy kept blowing on his food.

'Leave it alone for a while. If you burn your tongue, you won't enjoy it at all, and that will be a great pity,' she added. He was a good boy, typically energetic and overly fond of playing. But much of that energy was well spent on their excursions to the field. Sometimes in the evenings, when their meals were over, she would tell him about the old village of her childhood. He listened in great fascination to the stories of spirits visiting men and being hosted by them; he pestered Tola to repeat the story of the spirits dangling their legs on the rafters while singing courting songs. It was a picture that never failed to make him giggle. She would also tell him about his father and mother. The boy had a healthy curiosity about his parents but having had no memory of them, he was not acquainted with the bereavement that his grandmother always felt at the mention of them.

'Will I meet them someday?' he asked the first time she narrated their story to him. Initially, Tola did not know what to say.

'Namu, I do believe you will meet your parents when you die. In our religion, we believe that one day after we all die, we will surely meet all our loved ones again in the world of the dead. The elders say that life continues in the land of the dead very much the same way as we lived it here on earth. That is why when we die, we are buried with some seed-grains, so that we may carry it with us, and plant it and have food in our new homes. We always bury our dead with seed-grains. And we say that the dead travel along a road until they come to the place where the other dead are assembled.' She could not help feeling it was a rather lame explanation. Namu, however, was satisfied with her answer.

He was more interested in stories of his father when he was a lad like him. Did he go to the fields with his mother? Could he carry cucumbers in his basket like Namu did? Did he have a small dao like the one Namu had? His questions made Tola understand that Namu wanted to model himself on his father. Somehow that was important to his young mind, and she tried to tell him as much as she could recollect of his father as a young boy.

Chapter Two

Namu's father, Topong Nyakba, had been the only child of his parents. Before she conceived him, Tola and her husband had been married for many years without any signs of children. There were no miscarriages and interrupted pregnancies; Tola had simply not been able to conceive. She felt her barrenness as a constant burden pressing her down. The midwives she consulted prescribed different herbs to eat in different seasons, as well as secret women's rituals she could perform when the moon was receding. None of that had any effect on her fertility. She had even slept for several nights with the grain stones tied to her abdomen with a cloth. The grain stones were black in colour and kept by the granary or inside the grain containers because they made the grain multiply. Some people believed that they were potent enough to cure infertility in humans.

But for Tola, it had been a dismal failure, and all that she took away from that experience was a week of disturbed sleep. The fact of her childlessness made her distraught and she asked her husband to leave her and take another wife who could produce children to carry on his name. For if her husband had a male heir, it would ensure that his ancestral property would continue to remain in his family, and his position in the community house would be dignified by the mere fact that he had been able to father a son.

On the death of the head of the house, the families of men without male progeny forfeited all their property. Their houses and fields passed into the hands of the next of kin. A rich man who had no male offspring was allowed to set up sitting places of stone at prominent sites in the village. The sitting places would be called after his name, and it was the only avenue to ensure that his name would live on after he died; but this was a practice from which men with male heirs were discouraged. *The name of the man passes into the stones,* was the warning issued by the elders. In the next generations, parents would be very careful not to give their children the same name as that of the heirless man. In an agricultural society like theirs, infertility in animals and humans was considered a great curse, both to the family and to the community. Tongues would wag and people would try to bring back into public memory any taboo violations that had been committed by the man's ancestors as a possible reason for the fruitlessness. And in actual practice, the infertile man's name died with him. Tola cited all these reasons. But her husband refused to be persuaded to change his mind.

'Do you really think I would be happy to have a woman other than you as the mother of my children? Never. Tola, you are free to leave if you want to, but I will not be the one to ask you to leave.'

Topong Nyakba was born in winter. The whole village was astounded. Tola had hidden her pregnancy very well because she could not bring herself to believe the changes happening to her body. In the first trimester, when her monthly bleeding stopped, she thought it was because she was entering into the stage that women past their prime entered. She prepared to bear the veiled ostracism that accompanied barrenness. Women without children were automatically shut out of many of the activities that the village women took part in. Their shares of festival meat would be limited to one share; the blessings pronounced upon a household with progeny would pass hers by. She would voluntarily exclude herself when women sat together and discussed marriage prospects for their sons and daughters; she prepared to go through life as one ignorant of all the rituals that were to be performed before the marriages of one's children were contracted. And she would stop abruptly when she found herself humming the lullabies sung to put little ones to sleep.

But when three months had passed and her stomach thickened, and grew rounded as though she were putting on weight, she covered the protrusion with her body-cloth, and at night she lay awake for a long time, quietly stroking her rounded belly in the darkness, too amazed to believe it was real. And she would laugh a soundless laugh to herself, never telling a soul what was happening to her. Only when she was more than halfway past her pregnancy did she tell her husband about it after swearing him to secrecy. Then it became their shared treasure, and away from intrusive eyes she performed all the rituals that pregnant women were supposed to observe, and she abstained from eating all the foods that were taboo for them to eat.

Tola's condition became apparent to a few of her neighbours, but they couldn't bring themselves to believe it.

'Tola, you are finally putting on weight,' they teased.

'If I didn't know you better, I would say you were carrying a baby in there!' another woman laughed. Tola was a good-natured woman and they knew she wouldn't mind the reference to her barrenness. After all, she was not like the other barren women who had been put away by their husbands for younger, and more fertile wives.

'My husband feeds me very well,' Tola joked back. 'Rice and new cocoyam every evening. You should all try it too!' Her listeners laughed in unison. That was the manner in which she had directed the conversations, leading them away from any allusions to her pregnancy. It was in this way that Tola had taken every precaution to prevent people saying anything foolish or ill-meant over her condition. In private, she recollected everything her mother had taught her about childbirth a few days before her marriage, and she prepared herself well. She continued to jealously protect her pregnancy till the end, and when her pains finally started, her husband ran and fetched the astonished village midwife, as well as his married sister, to help; and between the three of them, a boy-child was safely delivered.

On the day Topong Nyakba was born there was hoarfrost on the ground. The wintry wind blew into the cracks in the split bamboo walls of their house, and they felt his cold breath lingering inside the dark rooms. In the winter months, they rarely let the fire go out. And now with the new addition to the household, it was important to match the warmth of the womb that had housed it for so many months, lest it find its new home inhospitable. Luckily, they had sufficient wood to last throughout the cold season.

The family had already brought the harvest home. Tola and her husband had filled the new grain baskets with this year's grain. The old grain baskets still held some portions of the remainder of last year's harvest. It was a good sign. It meant that the spirits were blessing them and in the coming years they would not see starvation. And now, the added blessing of a man-child served to complete the blessings of the household.

The baby boy was small and sickly. When Tola tried to put him to her breast, he cried feebly and refused to feed. The midwife bathed him with warm water, and held him close to make him stop whining. She told Tola not to worry as hunger itself would teach her son to feed. Her words came true quite quickly, and in no time the baby was learning to suckle, and it was not long before he began to seek milk and nourishment instinctively.

'He needs a good name,' Tola said to her husband. 'He needs a good, strong name. Let's not put off his naming; it would tempt the spirits.' She was referring to the belief that infants without names were more susceptible to being taken off by spirits.

Naming was a father's responsibility. Men were expected to be prepared beforehand. They were both familiar with the story of the man who neglected that task and found out only when it was too late. In the village, the story was repeated to generation after generation of a father who could not decide on a name for his new-born son. Day after day, he would rattle off the names of his ancestors, trying to choose the best of them all. He would linger over one but would be unable to settle on it, and pass on to the next venerable name. His wife nagged him to choose one, any one so that they would not have to run the risk of another night in a house with a nameless member. But for some inexplicable reason the man was unable to make up his mind. He made the excuse that if they started to use one, a better name might come to mind the next week, but by then they would have become so used to the first name that it was unlikely the new name would ever be used.

That evening, after dinner, there was a knock at the door. Thinking it might be their neighbour, the man got up and opened the door and a stranger walked in, gave him a knowing look, and headed straight for the bedroom. Smiling, he picked up the infant, who made no sound of protest. Still smiling, the stranger walked out of the house through the open door. At first, the parents were too dazed to comprehend what was happening.

Then the mother let out a piercing shriek, and only then did the father come to his senses and pick up his spear and go running into the night, shouting a challenge to the man who had stolen his child. But it was too late. There was no sign of the stranger and the child was never seen again. People always said that to keep a child unnamed was as good as throwing the door open for spirits to enter and steal the new member.

The villages to the north of them had an unusual practice. Everyone knew that the spirits would gather at the doorway of a house with a new-born, and wait with their ears against the walls, straining to capture the child's name the minute it was announced. Wise fathers would loudly call out a false name and the spirits would hear it and go away gleefully, thinking they had learned the infant's name. In later years, when the child ventured out into the woods, the spirits would call the child by that name, and they would try to entice the child away. The elders taught that it was so important to give a child a well-thought-out name that would protect it from spiritual harm.

Naming was a father's way of establishing ownership over the child. It would ensure that the child would not suddenly fall sick and die. Nevertheless, if an infant should become sick and linger between life and death for days, the parents would be told to give it another name. *His name is too heavy for him, he is not able to carry it*, the seer would say. *Give him a name that he can carry*, would be his advice. *Avoid words that make any reference to war or disputes*. Then a new name would be found quickly for the baby, and the family would begin to use it immediately. Grandparents learned to become adept at the art of naming, and they could be called upon at a moment's notice to help with suggestions for a new name. Many people swore that their children had been extricated from the jaws of death by christening them anew.

On the second day of his son's birth, Tola's husband declared, 'We will call him Topong Nyakba. It is a good and strong name. May his name help him overcome any physical weaknesses that could trouble him. May he build a good foundation for his generation and that of his children's generation and his grandchildren's.' It was the customary manner in which men gave names to their progeny. Good names, names with profound meanings were preferred for new babies, especially if they were male. The solemnity around the ceremony of naming had a very good reason. After all, naming a child carefully was as crucial as giving him the tools to lead a meaningful life.

So, Tola's son was named Topong Nyakba, and just as his father had stated, the baby grew strong and healthy. The winter months were short, and soon, not unlike a young sapling in Springtime, his limbs grew strong, and the muscles on his little body began to develop.

For a long time, the women of the village called him the miracle child. When they were questioned by outsiders as to why they called him such, they recounted the pregnancy of his mother who was over forty when it all happened, how she had laughed away their suspicions and allayed them, and defied fate with a baby born when the flame of hope had all but flickered out.

Topong Nyakba made his mother very happy. His parents never tried for a second child. They said it would have felt too close to greed or selfishness after the spirits had been so kind to them. He was a male-child who had the right to inherit his father's ancestral property. He would marry and have children of his own and both he and his children would look after his aged parents when that time came. Tola and her husband were more than satisfied with that.

Chapter Three

When Topong Nyakba turned fifteen, his father died in a hunting accident. It was winter and the grass was withered and dry on the ground. A group of men had gone out to hunt boars when one of the hunters voiced that it would be a good idea to make a bush fire and smoke out the animals. The men looked for and found places where they could wait to spear the animals as they came running out. The dry grass burnt easily spreading the fire to the dense vegetation where the boars were feeding. It didn't take long before the animals came squealing out and were speared by the hunters. But to their great alarm, the fire they started began to rage out of control. Their route of escape was blocked by burning trees and falling branches. The only man who escaped the inferno was the young son of the headman. Badly burnt, he crawled home to the village with his terrible news.

The forest fire was uncontrollable and they had to wait two days for its fury to be abated before they could collect the bodies of the men, or whatever was left of them. They were all buried beyond the village gate, as was the custom with unnatural deaths. To bury such within the village was to invite the same disaster to revisit them. Tola was beside herself with grief and would not be comforted. The disaster had come without any warning. Afterwards, she suffered nightmares of her husband screaming while flames consumed him. Topong Nyakba felt quite helpless to do anything, but he continued to tell her, 'Father would not want this for you.'

Tola mourned Topong Nyakba's father for a year. When her son had given up all hope of her recovery, she slowly came back to the land of the living. Tola was after all a seer's daughter. She never spoke of the things she had seen in dreams and visions and the voices that she had heard in her private moments. She emerged from her house one day, granite-faced, carrying her basket and her hoe, and headed to the field with her son. Her time of mourning was over; she vowed she would never let sorrow bow her to the ground again.

In Topong Nyakba's age-group, the boys greatly outnumbered the girls. The parents of the girls teased the boys saying, 'You will have to look for brides beyond the village. We don't have enough girls to go around for all of you.' In their age-group it was an unusual situation that there were eleven boys and just seven girls.

'Of course, the boys can marry girls from the age-group younger to them, but not from an older age-group,' a neighbour commented.

'Why is that?' Tola was surprised. 'I have never heard of such a taboo before.'

'It's not a taboo. But it is not good for the simple reason that an older woman would control her husband and turn him away from his parents, whereas a younger wife would respect and honour her husband's family.'

Tola laughed at the answer. But it became a matter of some anxiety that when all the members of Topong Nyakba's age-group were nearing the age to marry, the young men began to vie with each other for the attention of the girls.

Topong Nyakba said he was not interested in marrying. He was a hunter. He spent days in the forests hunting animals and bringing back meat to feed his mother and share with his relatives. In spite of his avowed disinterest in marrying, it was not very surprising to anyone that he eventually met his future wife in a village not far from his hunting grounds. Sechang was an attractive young woman with pleasing manners. Topong Nyakba's aunt sought permission from Sechang's parents, and they relented to the offer of marriage when they learned about his ancestry. Sechang's great-grandfather had been a famous warrior of their village, but had never been to war against Topong Nyakba's village. There was, therefore, no taboo against the two of them marrying. As a matter of fact, they were all members of the same tribe, and though Sechang's villagers spoke a different dialect from Topong Nyakba's, they had discovered that, with a little effort, they could understand one another. The taboos that applied to marriage were quite complicated. If the man and woman were from different villages, it was important to investigate village history to make sure there had been no feuding between their two villages in the past. Marrying into a former enemy village would mean both partners would violate the taboo on eating the food of an enemy. The consequence for such a violation was unnatural death.

One of the tales narrated repeatedly to reinforce this taboo was the unhappy love story of a personable young man who fell in love with a woman from another village. The two villages were separated by a river and the lovers had met in the dry months when the water level was low enough to allow the man to cross over to his lover's side. In the days that followed, the young couple contrived to spend the whole day together and parted only at sunset, with the man crossing back to his side of the river. The lovers met in this manner for many weeks. They had been told they would never be granted permission to marry, for neither set of parents would agree to it. So, they planned to run away and live their lives in another village where no one knew them. As the days passed, it became more and more dangerous for them to continue meeting. The woman's brothers had threatened to kill the man if they found them together. The couple planned their elopement and disregarded the fact that the water level was rising higher day by day.

It was a moonless night when the woman walked away from her village and headed to the river. She would wade across the river to her beloved waiting for her. When she reached the river bank, she saw a light burning on the other side. It was the signal that he was waiting, and her heart was calmed to see it. The woman stepped into the cold waters and began to cross the river. But when she was halfway across, the water rose to her neck and tried to strangle her, and she was very frightened and thought that she might die. She screamed her lover's name and he urged her onward, so she beat back the water and threshed her way to where he was. He pulled her out of the river and they rejoiced at their reunion. He led her down the path they would take to a village far from both their villages; it was there that they would start their lives together. It was a whole night and a whole day's walk away. There was a small house of thatch that they could use while they laboured to build their own house. Everything seemed to have worked out so well, they couldn't believe their luck. Joyfully, they went to sleep, planning to start work on their house the very next day.

But when morning came, they heard the villagers shouting and screaming from a distance. They opened the door to see what was happening, and found a great snake coiled at their door. The snake lunged at the woman and bit her to death. Her husband sprang at the snake and speared it, but as it was dying, the snake swung at the man and gave him a fatal bite. When the villagers reached the house, they found the two lovers lying dead, side by side. The seer said the spirit of the river had taken the form of a snake and killed them both for violating the taboo. This sad story was told in many villages to discourage intermarriage between villages that had formerly been at war with each other. The storyteller would end with a warning: *Breaking a taboo always breaks the violator.*

No hindrances were found to stop the marriage of Sechang and Topong Nyakba. Topong's gift to his in-laws was a two-pronged spear decorated with dyed goat's hair, and three cows. After the wedding feast Sechang's friends bid her goodbye, and she came to live with Topong Nyakba as his wife; she was a hard worker and Tola liked the respectful young woman who called her Mother. She had brought with her a bridal gift of fifty gourds of brew and thirty basketfuls of grain. They slaughtered a cow and feasted the villagers who, in turn, brought gifts of grain and seed-grain for the new family.

The newlyweds started their life together in their own house, a two-roomed house of bamboo walls and a new roof of thatch. They tilled the fields together with Tola and harvested enough grain before the year was over. When the new year began, and the season of birdsong and clear night skies arrived, Sechang felt the stirrings of new life within her. It was a good beginning. Her mother had impressed upon her that it was a blessing to be fertile. Namu was born about a year into their marriage, and Tola wiped away tears of joy when she saw her grandchild. It brought back memories of Topong Nyakba's birth and the long years of barrenness she had endured. 'Let there be more children,' she prayed. Her husband's name and her son's name would live on now, she thought, as she felt gratitude surge up in her heart.

After Namu's birth, Tola spent the early days in caring for the baby and his mother, bathing the infant, and cooking meals for them. She divided her days between looking after them and finishing the rest of the labour in the fields that were getting ready to be harvested. But it was not long before Sechang was up and about, and taking over her own duties again.

'Mother, I am strong now. I don't want you working so much anymore. Look, if I tie Namu on my back, I can do almost everything.' Sechang used a wide band of cloth to secure the baby on her back, and she went about her tasks of fetching water and wood, and even cooking food for the family.

Tola admired her industriousness, but also warned, 'Just don't overtire yourself. Work is always waiting for a woman.'

Once she saw how capable her daughter-in-law was, Tola retreated to her own house. She had done the same with Topong Nyakba, carrying him to the fields and back and getting her work done. Only when he was too heavy to carry, did she leave him in the care of an old widow while she and her husband worked at their field. But by the time Topong Nyakba was three years old, he could follow his parents back and forth.

Tola and Sechang took turns carrying Namu, and before the year was out, they managed to finish the field work. Every evening, Sechang and Topong would eat their evening meals in Tola's house. The older woman would have a fire ready that gave a welcoming warmth. The winter months were upon them and only a good fire could keep their houses warm. The earthen floors trapped the cold air and left their houses bleak and frigid. It was the fireplace in the heart of the kitchen that provided heat for the whole house. Tola had a mat for Namu to sleep on while the adults cooked food and ate their meals together.

In these days of waiting for the harvest, the villagers guarded the fields from birds and wild animals. Several of them spent nights at the fields so that they could make a jangling noise early in the morning and chase birds away. At night, they kept the outside fires burning to discourage bigger animals from approaching the fields and destroying the grain. Topong spent many nights guarding the grain in both fields. This sacrifice was the only way to ensure that a year's worth of human labour would not be consumed by animals.

Chapter Four

The harvest was brought in when there was a period of excellent weather. It was hard work, but no one complained because they were happy to have food stores for another year. Before the harvest could commence, the seer had announced the festival dates so that the villagers could prepare for the harvest festival. It was a time to give thanks to the creator for a good harvest and a plague-free year. Young people who were betrothed would marry during the festival week. The general rule was that marriages took place after the harvest when all field work was over. In the two or three months of rest after the harvest, newly-weds were encouraged to build their houses, if they had not already done so, as they could get help from other members.

Tola tried hard to join in the festive mood that always infected the village after the harvest. The harvest festival was not just a time of thanksgiving but also a time of celebration. It came at the end of a long year of toiling in the fields, in the sun and rain. People gave thanks to the creator-deity, and they solicited blessings for the new cultivation at hand. Already the younger members were forming groups and practising songs and dances for the festival. Beside the furrowed fields wild sunflowers were blooming in abundance. Children liked to bring the yellow flowers home and stick them into the split bamboo walls of their houses. Someone had given baby Namu a flower and he had promptly put it in his mouth.

Tola looked around her and watched all the gaiety, and felt a deep emptiness rise up inside her. She recognised that feeling; it had come the day that her husband had gone hunting and never returned. It had come the morning her mother took ill and suddenly died in the evening. Why was it rising up now when everything had become well again and she could count herself fortunate in her son and his family?

Tola was a dream receiver like her father before her. He was old but his powers were still potent, and as seer, his dreams were significant ones for the village. She could never become seer on his death, because she was a woman. The mantle would pass on to her cousin, the next male relative. Hence, she tried to ignore the disturbing dreams that she had been having lately, attributing it to her husband's ghastly death many years ago and what she had gone through after that. She wanted to believe it was no more than a revisitation of the worst time in her life. What else could it be? The screaming women of her dreams were none other but her younger self, widowed and screaming her loss. The men in her dreams speared in their beds were surely the spirits of her husband and his friends eaten by the hungry flames. And the voices singing the dirges for the dead that she often heard at night must be what the widows had sung when they learnt the fates of their men. She kept reasoning in this manner and never knew that the gift had now passed from her father to her, and the dreams were not visitations from the past, but warnings for a future time not long from now.

After the harvest was over, Tola had not rested well at all. Sleep eluded her most nights; On the nights that sleep came, all she could remember was a long sequence of dreaming. The sleepless nights left her fatigued and confused. But she did not wish to pry into the secrets her dreams carried. Life had given her too many unkind lessons; she had no desire to unfurl any others.

Tola also chose to ignore the process of seership. There had been great female seers in the past; not in her village but in far off settlements that no one ever travelled to unless they needed guidance on a situation so grave that the wisdom of their village seer was not enough. In such cases, the village seer would himself direct the person to travel to the villages that were ruled by female seers. *Your problem begs a feminine answer*, the seer would say. *No male seer should presume to substitute his own wisdom for that of a woman's.*

They were all familiar with the story of the man who had approached the female seers to help him resolve the question of custody over his son. Early in his marriage, the man discovered that he was unable to have children with the woman he had married; to prevent him taking another wife, the woman agreed to bear the child of a forest spirit. After some months, she gave birth to a baby boy, and all was well. But when the child grew older and learned to talk, he began to complain saying that there was a man who always followed him around, and tried to snatch him away from his playmates. It was the spirit father. The village seer sent both the man and the spirit father to the village of the female seers.

They set off early the next morning and arrived at the village in the afternoon. When they stated their case, they were told to wait their turn outside the house of the female seers. After a long wait, an elderly woman appeared at the great wooden door and beckoned both the fathers to draw closer. She was tall and very thin, her thinness making her appear even taller. She wore an unadorned black body-cloth, and stood at the entrance of the house staring at the pair with unsmiling eyes that seemed to penetrate right through them. With anger barely concealed, she burst out, 'You are here to ask who the boy belongs to? Ha! The conceit of it! Mark my words: he belongs to the womb that housed him, and to the breast that nursed him, but most of all, he belongs to himself. He is not anyone's property. Stop your squabbling and together bring him up in the best way possible!' She turned on her heel and went back inside the house. That was the end of the matter. The two applicants exchanged sheepish glances and made their separate ways back.

Tola never saw herself taking on a similar role and using her wisdom to guide the many village decisions. She did acknowledge that her dreams were a result of her having seer blood. But to take that any further would be too presumptuous on her part. That was what she always told herself, so the revelations given to her stayed unshared.

The harvest festival was a happy one, more so because of the many marriages celebrated in that year. Young brides went home to their new homes. They were from the age-group below Topong Nyakba's age-group. More households were a matter of rejoicing for the whole village: their numbers would increase when the young couples began to have children, swelling the community in a natural manner. The new moon was out, stars gleamed in the night skies, and courting songs drifted out from the *morungs*; dancing groups were in no hurry to go home yet, and there was no reason to believe that their fortunes would be changed in just a few hours.

Chapter Five

The attacks came in the dead of night, when the men were sound asleep, drunk on new brew, and the women were dreaming of the bright lives ahead of them. The enemy warriors scaled the village walls at its weakest points, broke down the bamboo doors, speared the sleeping householders, and made their escape. Too late the seer realised what was happening, and he ran outside and shouted warnings. His cries managed to wake some of the survivors, but one of the intruders turned around, threw a spear at him and silenced him.

Tola woke up thinking her dreams had followed her into her waking hours. She could hear voices, screams of women and children crying. Running out, she saw the shadowy figures scaling the wall and running off into the night. Then she knew the worst had happened.

'Father!' she screamed and ran to the seer's house. The body slumped over in the compound was her father's. The spear had dropped off his back and blood was oozing out from the great wound. Tola instinctively covered the wound with her hand but the warm blood seeped through her fingers. She quickly pulled off her head-cloth, folded it into a thick pad and covered the wound. That seemed to help a little. She pulled her father's right hand over her shoulder and with all her strength she dragged him into the house and laid him halfway across the bed. She then pulled him aright and tended to his wound. It had gone deep and blood kept oozing out.

Working quickly, Tola lit a wormwood torch, and she went through the salves and herb pastes that her father had mixed together and set aside for his patients. All her life she had watched her father making the herbal pastes, combining potent herbs with curative herbs and producing different cures. She knew exactly what she was looking for. Tola grabbed the paste and took it back to her father, carefully peeled off the cloth and applied a thick layer over the wound. The blood ran off the sides of the paste and into the bedclothes. She kept applying more of the paste into the gash until the bleeding subsided and was kept in abeyance. He was not conscious, but he was breathing evenly. At least the bleeding had been stopped. She found a long strip of gauze cloth that she folded into a pad, and using strips of plaster she secured it over his wound.

When his breathing became more regular, her thoughts turned to the others. Topong and Sechang! And Namu! How were they? Could she leave her father and run over and check? Outside the house, the sobbing of women grew louder and Tola's heart constricted at the sound. Why hadn't Topong run over to check that she was safe? She shut her mind out to the idea of the unthinkable and ran from her father's house to her son's. But it had happened. Topong Nyakba and Sechang had both been speared as they slept. They were both dead. Tola began to howl. Her howling woke up little Namu who had slept through the horror.

The days after the attack on their village were very hard. With heavy hearts, the survivors buried their dead. Fathers buried sons, sons buried mothers and grandfathers buried grandchildren. The dirges were heard from morning till evening, and sometimes in the middle of the night, when a bereaved one would wake up and remember her loss, a low dirge would begin as she mourned her loved ones again. Then there would be no sleep for the others.

They had lost their headman, Chingmak. The old seer, Tola's father, was alive, but only just, the spear in his back having left a gaping wound that was festering. The other survivors besides Tola and Namu were Chongshen, the seer's nephew and his family; Chongshen's newly wedded son and his wife were among the survivors. Beshang, an old widower, his son and family; two elderly widows and the headman's widow; Choba, the headman's son with his wife and child. Nine households in a village of twenty-two houses. Theirs had never been a big village by any standards but it was a peaceful settlement founded by their ancestors, known for their fastidious observance of the *genna* days and rituals that accompanied all the activities of the agricultural year. When the news of the attack reached the neighbouring villages, it came as a great shock. They expected that the survivors would abandon the village and migrate or that they would find a new site to settle. It was unheard of that people would continue to live in a village when a tragedy of such great proportions had occurred within its walls. It meant that the village had no potency to protect its members.

Villages sacked by enemy warriors, destruction by earth-quakes, lightning strikes that set fires and resulted in mass destruction – these were some of the reasons for which villages were immediately abandoned. It was also a taboo to continue living in a village that had had its granaries destroyed by swarms of rodents. A day's walk away from Tola's village was a village that had to be abandoned because two brothers had killed each other fighting over their father's lands. Blood-letting between near relations was the greatest taboo recognised by any village. The spirits of the brothers gave the villagers no rest and, in the end, the headman found another site to settle. The abandoned village of the brothers continued to be haunted by the two spirits. People studiously avoided travelling past it, choosing to take a circuitous path instead.

In the weeks that followed the great tragedy, that was the question on everyone's minds and hearts. They gathered together every day and each time they met they talked about it. Should they leave? Why wait for another attack to wipe them all out? Could they bear the burden of complete annihilation? Yet, if they settled elsewhere, would not the name of their village die out? The older members felt burdened by this question.

The seer put a stop to all their doubts. He was unable to leave his bed as his wound was so severe. Tola constantly tended her father, her grandson tied to her back. The seer was in great pain as the spear tip had punctured his right lung. He kept coughing up blood and every time he coughed, he thought his heart would burst. 'Let me go now,' he pleaded between each burst of coughing. Fatigued, he would lean back in bed, his face to the wall. That was when he saw the vision.

'Tola, Tola,' he began to call weakly. Tola never left her father's side. Even when she was making food in the kitchen, she would put her pot on the fire and check in on her father.

'Father, I am here,' she answered.

He was dying, she could see that so clearly now.

'Listen to me,' he whispered.

'Don't strain yourself, Father,' she chided.

'No, you have to listen to me. It's a message for the village.'

Tola knew when to keep silent before her stern father.

'I have seen a vision, tell them that. Rebuild the village. Do not abandon it. The massacre is not the worst thing it has seen. There is something much bigger coming. The village has a great destiny. But if the survivors abandon the village, it cannot fulfil its destiny, and the punishment for that will follow you all your lives. Tell the people about this vision, tell them to obey because obedience is the only thing that will save the village. Tell them, tell them!' He fixed his dilated eyes on her before the light died in them.

Tola reached over and closed her father's eyes, carefully pulled off the bedclothes and washed his emaciated body before covering it with a new body-cloth. After this was done, she went to the new headman's house to tell him so that he might inform the others of the death of the seer. She then went back to her father's house, chanting a dirge, dry-eyed. The few men that were left beat the log drum to announce the death of the seer. Soon, the other householders came and joined Tola in mourning her seer father. A night long vigil was held, and the men got up in turns, and as was their custom they spoke their praises of the seer. The next afternoon the seer was buried beyond the village gate. The old seer had been one of the most powerful seers for miles around. Many from neighbouring villages used to seek his guidance. The funeral was attended by these supplicants who came to join in mourning him. In the absence of male progeny, the seer's nephew performed the rituals for the dead.

Choba, the headman's son had succeeded his father as headman. After the funeral, Tola told him about the vision her father had seen. She conveyed how adamant her father had been that the village should not be abandoned. Choba was a wise man, he knew the folly of disregarding the guidance provided by the spirits. He called the people together and spoke to them as a father would address his children,

'We will rebuild our village.' There was a quiet conviction in his voice. 'We will not move elsewhere, but we will live on here and tend the graves of our ancestors, and when challenges come in the future, may we not be found wanting. To run away like cowards or to remain and live our lives with dignity and courage – that is the choice before us, and we know what to choose. My people, never forget the village that birthed you. *Shumang Laangnyu Sang*, River Rock village. Our ancestors came here because they were given a dream of a great rock beside a river. The creator deity promised them that they would be great like the rock, and that they would be sought after like a river is sought for its life-giving water. Our village has always given wisdom to others which is the reason why people come from great distances to take the counsel of our seers.

'We will remain here, and grow strong again like the rock guardian of our village. We will not allow *Shumang Laangnyu Sang* to die. It will live to fulfil its destiny.'

In the days that followed, the villagers began going back to their fields, working the land and honouring the spirits when it was the time to do so. Their lives would never be the same again. But they would not give in to despair. Working the fields was a movement towards life and it comforted them as it was knowledge that was familiar to all of them.

Chapter Six

Tola had very little memory of the weeks and months that followed. She had buried her father and her son and daughter-in-law. All their dead were buried beyond the village gate as was the custom for any member who had fallen in war, or suffered an unnatural end. The old headman's house was one of the first houses to be attacked. He had been killed immediately. That his son, Choba, should become the new headman was a unanimous decision. It was to be expected that his father would have trained him to take over the role of headman after him. Choba's house lay next to his father's but each house had its own compound. Tola's cousin Chongshen became the new seer. He was much younger than her. But he was the closest male relative of the seer.

Of the survivors, Beshang, the widower, had his house at the end of the village; that was probably why he had escaped the attack. The houses where every member was killed were the houses on the eastern side of the village. All villages clung to the belief that building one's house there made the children healthy as the first rays of the sun always fell on these houses in the east. The men of title had their great houses with their elaborate jutting roofs on the eastern side of the village. The skulls of cattle that had been killed by them to feast the village were hung under the roofs in long rows. Each of these houses had been attacked and its inhabitants killed. The village was left without a single household of title-takers. .

Tola felt that the return to living had taken place too rapidly; she had not been given time to mourn her dead properly, and she was right. She more than anyone knew that death was an inevitable part of life, but when it had taken off three at a time, how was one to mourn? Releasing all that grief could have killed the mourner and she had her young grandson to think of now. Her life had never been her own, now less than ever. None of the survivors were in any position to comfort each other. But of them all, the two widows were the first to recover. Sungmo, the older widow was childless. She had stepped in to help care for Namu so that Tola could look after her dying father, and even after his death, she continued to help Tola with her grandson.

This was how the village rebuilt itself, in the way that the stronger members gave of themselves to care for the weaker ones and share their burdens. Every morning, Sungmo went to house after house and in her gentle way, helped light the fire for them and boiled water for their morning meals. The recipients of her care responded by making the effort to participate in daily living again. The widower Beshang shared his grain with every surviving house. They had grain too, but they accepted his gift, realising that it was his way of extending love. The survivors rallied around bravely, and slowly the village came out of its stupor. They would never again laugh so freely as before; they would be cautious in the evening hours making sure every member was safely back before shutting the gate, and they would always remember to greet each other kindly.

The village walls were repaired. That was one of the first things the men attended to with their new headman. In fact, they made the walls much higher and cut away the earth around them ensuring that they became impossible to scale. They also planted nettles and brambles at the base of the walls so that any intruder would get an unpleasant shock.

In these days of becoming a village again, they began to eat their meals together. They cooked food in their own homes, but when it was meal time, each household brought their pots to the square, and shared their food with their neighbours. There was something healing in the action. They were coming together as a family, as a community in the truest sense. The sharing of food bonded them, and they got to know each other's tastes, likes and dislikes, and as time passed, a few mild jokes were hesitantly made around the food table. That was how Tola knew their healing had begun.

And all of them kept the old seer's words in their hearts: *The massacre is not the worst thing the village has seen. There is something much bigger coming. If you abandon the village, it cannot fulfil its destiny. Be obedient because obedience is the only thing that can save the village.*

If there was something coming that was bigger than the massacre, how would that be, they wondered. Was the massacre that reduced their village from twenty-two households to nine not bad enough? How could the survivors rise again to fight off the next attack? These were their first questions. But in the days following the massacre, they had found something else – a profound sense of tenderness. That tenderness was at the true heart of living. Life was no longer defined by the practical duties that a man and a woman had to fulfil. There was so much more to life than merely performing ritual after ritual and looking after the religious regularity of observing *genna* days every month. Even Tola had to admit that life went far beyond the continuance of a man's name. The hitherto unimportant and the neglected had now become the important. And they would endeavour to take care of it.

Beshang became the self-appointed storyteller of the village. After the community meal, Beshang told them this story: 'There was once a village of ten warriors feared by all other villages feuding against them. The ten men were the fiercest in the territory and no foe had managed to withstand them. They were undefeated in battle and word spread that their valour came from the fact that they were half-man, half-spirit. How this could happen was if the men had been fathered, not by human fathers, but by spirits. All ten had taken the names of the men whom they each called father, but who was to know if these men had actually fathered them? By and by, the stories came out that one warrior had been sired by a tree spirit when his mother had been herb gathering. Another man was believed to have had a wolf spirit for a father. He was especially ferocious on the battlefield and was reputed to have killed the greatest number of enemy warriors. A third warrior had had a weretiger for a grandfather. And so it went on, and the belief spread that the ten were invincible because of their spirit origins.

'The village of the ten warriors was protected by this story and became great and steadily powerful. The day came when they grew bored of protecting their hearths against others; they felt strong enough to go out and plunder enemy villages and enrich themselves thus. And their fame had grown and grown: who would be so foolhardy as to fight them back? The ten warriors were counselled by men greedy to profit by their alliances with them. The seer stepped in and advised caution; more than that, he forbade them from going on the warpath against villages that were now paying tribute to them. But the warriors were told that the seer was cowardly and need not be heeded. So, they went out and attacked their enemies, beginning with the weakest of them. They took that village easily, plundered it and burnt it and went on to the next until finally they came to the strongest village.

'Back in their ancestral village, the seer warned the people to get ready to leave if they did not want to be annihilated. A few families obeyed him and followed him carrying with them the items they would need to start a new village – utensils and clothing, agricultural implements and some seed-grain. The families of the ten warriors with their advisors stayed back.

'Meanwhile, the ten warriors were facing the greatest challenge of their lives. The village they had attacked had walls of stone. It was iron-like. Its warriors greatly outnumbered them, and as they rushed at them in a counter attack, the ten warriors found themselves completely abandoned by their supporters. They were all speared to death, and after that, their enemies made sure their ancestral village was destroyed so thoroughly that no one could ever find any trace of it on earth again.'

Beshang had come to the end of his story. He looked at each one in his audience. They were all waiting for his next words. He had timed it well. 'Never harbour pride. Pride destroys everything. There is no protection against the spirit of pride and it does not matter whether you are a human or a spirit, pride will always find you out and consume you utterly.'

The widower was the oldest male. They might not always obey him, but they would all respectfully listen when he told them a story.

Chapter Seven

Tola tended Namu jealously. They left for the field in the morning, sometimes with Sungmo accompanying them, and the women looked after him in turns. Tola provided her grandson all the firmness that a father would have been expected to give, and all the love that a mother could have given. He wanted for nothing. And he grew up loving the wise woman who could answer his every question. When he started to talk, he called her *Kunyu*, my mother. But Tola quickly corrected that, and the young boy learned to call her *Abi nyu*, grandmother. She taught him all the bird names on their way to the field. By the time he was three years old, he knew the river names and the field names along the route they daily took.

Namu was a growing boy. When he turned three, he no longer wanted to be carried. His grandmother allowed him to walk beside her to the field, lugging his own little basket. In the beginning, he wanted to explore every bit of the world that had opened up to him by his new-found mobility. Tola was firm with him, and they soon established a strict routine dictating that field work was a priority, but once that was done, they could roam in the woods close to the terrace fields, picking berries and finding birds' nests.

Tola's wooden hut stood in the middle of her field. Everyone had similar huts where they spent the night if there was too much field work to do. The simple wooden door was never locked; Tola would knot a rope around the ring on the wall and tighten it round the other ring attached to the door. It was enough to prevent animals from entering the shed. They kept all their agricultural tools in the hut. In a corner were the empty seed bags, folded and kept away to be reused. In another corner was a bed covered with jute bags and coarse blankets. It was not comfortable but Tola would argue that if she was spending a night in the field, it was not to seek comfort. It was because there was work to do and there was nothing better than being able to sleep at the hut and start working early in the morning.

Namu was very happy to spend nights there. He loved to watch the stars come out; they seemed closer and bigger than ever. The sounds of the outdoors were different from the village sounds. The forest was never completely silent. Insect noises and animal calls were louder in the night time. In the summer months smaller animals like frogs croaked through the night. In the rainy season, bears sometimes sought shelter in abandoned sheds, and in the cold months of October, November and December, they could hear deer barking near the field. Sometimes, packs of jackals roamed near the fields and howled in unison. Namu's ears would prick up when he heard the jackals howling from a distance.

'Do jackals eat people?' Namu asked his grandmother.

'I've never heard of anything like that,' Tola answered. 'Don't worry, they sound terrible when they howl but they actually like to eat chickens, not people. In any case, we have a good fire going and no animal will come near a fire.'

The fireplace in the hut was quite simple; it was there to serve a practical purpose and not an aesthetic one. It was just three cooking stones of roughly the same height placed close together to support a pot. There was space beneath for a fire to be made by pushing small pieces of dry wood between the stones. When they were burning nicely, Tola would place a big piece of wood atop the flames.

From time to time, Tola performed the ritual to honour the cooking stones. At such times, Namu would sit in a corner and watch his grandmother sprinkle rice-brew on the three cooking stones and talk to them as though she were talking to a human being. She finished by mumbling a prayer that was quite incoherent to any listener.

'Why do you give the cooking stones rice-brew and talk to them?' Namu asked when he was older.

'Hush, they will hear you,' she cautioned. 'I am honouring the cooking stones so we can get a good harvest,' she said in a low voice. And because of what she had told him, Namu was very careful not to do anything offensive around the cooking stones. He hoped they would forgive him for the time when he had urinated at the fireplace because he had been scared to go outside.

Tola's daughter-in-law Sechang had come from a village where they did not use cooking stones. She said she had never heard of the ritual. On the second day of her marriage, she found some red soil, dug it up and carried it to her kitchen, mixed it with water and moulded a hearth out of the wet clay. She then laid two lengths of metal across the hearth and made fire beneath it. After that, Tola taught her to perform the ceremony of the cooking stones over her hearth. It was important because it was part of the ritual of thanksgiving to the creator for the harvest they would get from their labours – the sacrament to ensure the grain would provide food for the whole year.

The fields closest to the village were less than an hour's walk away. The last of the fields lying on the borders of the next village were much further away. The valley areas were covered with the fields that lay adjoining each other's. In the early part of the year, the villagers tilled their *jhum* fields on hill slopes. But once there was a little rain to soften the soil, all of them began work in the terrace fields. Next to the fields were the woods. Bears liked to wander into the fields if they planted maize along the field borders, so people had stopped that practice. Nowadays they sowed maize only on the hill slopes.

Field work was arduous and lasted all day, with a brief pause for eating lunch. The workers would stop when the crickets started their shrill singing. They called it their going-home-time songs.

The crickets had begun singing when Namu and Tola gathered up their things to go home. Tola stoppered her gourd of rice-brew and put it in an upright position in her basket. She then added twigs and small pieces of wood and bark. Most people carried back wood from the fields to the village. Atop the wood, she placed a bundle of Indian Pennywort that she had gathered earlier.

Namu held out his little basket. 'What shall I carry back?'

'You can carry some wood,' she said as she piled little pieces of bark into his basket. 'We can make use of all that to make a nice fire when we get home.' He beamed at her words.

On the way back they were joined by other field-goers and they chatted about their labours, how much they had got done, and how much was now left. Tola looked for Sungmo as they were crossing her field, but there was no sign of the widow.

'Sungmo!' she called out but there was no reply. She must have gone home early, Tola concluded, and forgot about it as they neared the village. Once they were at home, she became preoccupied with fetching water for their baths and cooking the evening meal.

However, she saw that she had made too much food for the two of them. 'I'll take some over to Sungmo now,' she said to herself. But Namu was tired and hungry so she ladled a portion into a container, and the two of them ate the rest of it. He was half asleep when they finished eating. Tola managed to hoist him on her back, securing him with the carrying-cloth. Next, she picked up the container of food and headed to Sungmo's house.

The widow's house was dark and silent. 'Sungmo!' she called out at the entrance. There was no response. From the doorway Tola noticed that there was no fire burning in the hearth; it looked like it had not been lit the whole day.

'Sungmo,' she called again. When there was no reply, she called louder, and made her way inside. Sungmo was lying in bed, and when she heard Tola's voice she moaned by way of answer.

'I didn't feel well at all today,' she mumbled apologetically.

'Don't you worry about that. Here, I have brought you some food.'

'I'm not hungry, nevertheless thank you for bringing it.' Her voice was very weak; Tola reached out and felt her forehead. It was cold and clammy to the touch.

'You don't have a fever.'

'No, I'm just tired, don't worry. I'm old enough to be tired on some days.' She tried to laugh but the effort made her cough instead.

'You can eat some food a little later. We're staying with you tonight,' Tola said decisively, but Sungmo protested.

'It's not a problem at all,' Tola laughed. 'At least it will be more comfortable than the jute bags I have been lying on in the hut.' Tola laid Namu down on the next bed. She made Sungmo eat a little food and after she had made sure her friend was comfortable, they both lay down to sleep.

Sungmo died peacefully in the morning. There had been no struggle. Just like the way she had lived her life. Even in death, she had gone so quietly it was as though she hadn't wanted to trouble anyone with her dying. One moment she was talking to Tola, describing her dream, and in the next moment her eyes closed and her gentle heart stopped beating.

It was a sad time for the village. But Sungmo was old, much older than Tola. She was past eighty and had no children of her own. She had no relatives in other villages either so there was no one to inform of her passing. Her house would be shuttered after the body was taken to the burial ground. The women folded her best clothes and buried them with her along with a small bag of different seed grains so she should have something to start her next life with. After the burial, the women covered the little shed over her grave with the long leaves of a wild fern, replacing the withered leaves with fresh ones every week. They did this for many weeks. It was a custom to show that the dead was fondly remembered by the living.

Chapter Eight

With Sungmo gone, Tola became the second oldest person in the village. She would be seventy-five in the summer. Her father had been 90 when he died. The old headman, Choba's father, had been in his eighties at the time the massacre happened. Beshang was older than her by three years, but he was not from the line of seers.

The attack had taken off all the really old people in their village. Their real loss was to be a village bereft of the wisdom of the old. There was no way to fill in that gap. They would just have to remember what they had been taught when they were younger and try to live life with that knowledge. But Tola had an uneasy feeling that more was expected of them, of her especially. It was not unusual that the men would come to consult her when they were confused about a ritual or a decision that would affect the lives of the community. She never took advantage of it. Chongshen was the official seer. It would not do for her to undermine his authority or wisdom. On any occasion when she was called upon to share some spiritual insight on a problem, she began her sentences with, 'My father said' or 'My father used to perform this ritual,' totally avoiding ascribing the source of the knowledge to herself. She never told anyone of the many dreams and waking dreams that she had received. When Sungmo was alive, she had confided in her. Sungmo had been convinced that

Tola was supposed to be the village seer after her father, and urged her to share the revelations with the headman. But Tola continued to resist the idea adamantly. Chongshen, on his part, never lost the opportunity to remind people that the destiny of the village lay upon his shoulders, just as much as it did upon the headman's.

'I can never cross the borders of our village,' he had been overheard explaining to the village youths. 'In my office as priest and seer, if I crossed the village forests and placed my foot upon the lands of our neighbour villages, my action would expose the village to all sorts of spiritual and physical attacks. It is because I carry the virtue of the village in my person, you see.' Ever since he had been made seer, he strove to look dour and long-suffering. But the truth was that Chongshen secretly enjoyed portraying himself as a martyr for the safety of the village. He had always wanted to be seer. There was some truth to the story that when he was a young man, he had been caught spying on his uncle the seer while the latter was undertaking a ritual of sacrifice for the community. He admitted to it, but also insisted it was done out of his eagerness to learn all that he could to help the village.

Tola had never wanted to burden the seer with what had been happening to her. Yet she found it heavy to bear on her own. She had to tell someone what was happening to her, someone she trusted completely. The visitations had begun while Sungmo was still alive. The first came in the middle of the night, when Tola was abruptly woken by something, and she lay in bed with all her senses alert. All on a sudden, she saw a man noiselessly enter her house. Alarmed, she tried to sit up and scream but her voice came out as a strangled cry. The man was dressed like a warrior. He stepped forward and covered her mouth. When he let go, she could neither speak nor move throughout the length of time it lasted for her to take in all that he was showing her. She had fallen back into bed, and lain there powerless before the intruder. Tola quickly realised that the warrior was no man, but a spirit emissary. There was a scene that he repeatedly showed her. She recognised the village as her village, but bigger and with more people in it. She did not recognise the children that flitted in and out of the square but with a shock she recognised some of the older people; they were her neighbours, only they appeared much older.

As she watched, a giant tiger leaped out into the sky and began to eat the sun. Tola screamed silently at the sight, but it would not stop until it had finished its meal. When it was over, a great darkness fell upon the village, and the sounds of children crying and people shouting grew so loud that she struggled to put her hands over her ears and lower her head. 'Stop! Stop!' she silently pleaded. Without any warning, the noises ceased, and when she looked up again, the man was gone, the vision had come to an end.

Tola wondered what it all meant. She dearly wanted to ask someone about it. When she found the courage to tell Sungmo, not leaving out any detail, the older woman said, 'It must be some great secret in the future which you are being allowed to witness. Don't be afraid. Next time, make your heart strong and watch on. You must learn more.'

'If there is a next time.' Tola was not sure if she was ready for another visitation.

'I'm sure there will be a next time. You are fortunate to be chosen to receive this knowledge. Stiffen your heart and step into it. It's important for all of us,' Sungmo encouraged her.

And there was a next time. The spirit emissary returned exactly a month after the first vision. This time Tola did not protest; she pressed her fears down and lay back trying to take in every detail. It was the same vision of their village, and people going about their work as usual. She paid careful attention and could see that there were actually only a few people in the village. The majority were in the fields working, and the coming of the darkness created great panic amongst them. She saw them running back to the safety of the village, stumbling in the dark, their lungs hurting from the unaccustomed exertion. They ran blindly, holding out their hands in front of them, pressing down the panic in their hearts. As they ran forward, the village became visible because there were two or three bamboo torches burning. But even when they reached the safety of the village, the darkness never lifted.

What would happen? How would they get the sun back? The vision was, however, ended for the time being and she had to wait until the next visit. Sungmo was already dead and buried when the third visit came.

The darkness was all pervasive. Tola could not see anything. The skies were pitch-black and the darkness over the land was all encompassing. Whether she kept her eyes open or closed, there was no difference. At one point, Tola put her hands to her eyes to check that she had kept them open. She could see nothing. It was as though she were inside the interior of a cave. However, she could hear voices singing in a melancholic manner – they were dirges for the dead. *So, people would die at this time,* she concluded from the sounds of mourning. People were being named in the dirge singing, but the voices were indistinct and Tola could not make out who would die during the darkness. Dirge followed dirge – she counted but lost track of how many dirges were chanted. There was no letting up. When the vision was over, she fell into a deep, dreamless sleep.

Tola spent her days thinking of the visions. What she could gather out of it all was that a day of great destruction was coming to their village. Would that be the end of their village? She had heard dirge singing, the monotonous chanting for the dead. Would the population die out one by one in the darkness? What a terribly oppressive thought. Surely, they did not deserve such a fate. Tola was deeply troubled by the knowledge she was being given. Her memory was jogged by a story she had heard in childhood: *Tiger and Man and Spirit were brothers. But Tiger was jealous of man and always sought to harm him. One day Tiger committed a taboo and they could no longer live together as one family. Tiger went to live in the woods, Man in the open plains and Spirit is Spirit. He lives everywhere. Man is peaceable, but Tiger is not. He wants to eat the sun and when the light of the sun is gone, he will eat all of Man's children. Everyone must hide on the day Tiger eats the sun.*

Was this childhood tale told with foreknowledge, she wondered? But what would one do with this kind of foreknowledge? People needed to be instructed on how to make atonement if some taboos had been violated.

The thought that she should go with the information to the seer, Chongshen, had occurred to her more than once. But she stopped herself when she remembered that if anything was going to happen to the village, the seer was the right channel to receive that pre-knowledge, not a widow. True she was the old seer's daughter and the blood of seers ran in her veins because her grandfather and great-grandfathers had all been seers, but Chongshen was the official seer and he often shared spiritual information that he had received in the night. It was never, however, anything on this scale.

Chongshen as seer proclaimed the days for seed-sowing and harvesting, and the days for the festivals to begin. He performed all the major rituals, be it for a household or for the village as a whole. And he made a point, indeed, of letting everyone know that he avoided any travel beyond the village territory because it was said that a seer should never leave the village. If he did so, the village would surely be visited by epidemics and even famine. Tola was apprehensive that Chongshen might think she was trying to compete with him if she revealed all that she was being given access to. She had never shared with anyone the harrowing dreams she had experienced before the massacre. If she recollected them, she pressed down the guilt that rose up to accuse her of failing to save lives by not speaking up. But even if she had shared them, would they have taken heed of her dreams? Would they have listened to a woman? A widow?

The third visitation came after the harvest. Months had passed since the last time, and Tola had concluded that was all she was going to be shown. She and Namu had brought in their harvest, finished the rituals for protection of the harvest, and prayed their grain would be long-lasting and feed them throughout the next agricultural year. Young Namu followed her around the house as she sprinkled rice brew on the house posts and on the woven grain containers, propitiating the spirit of the house and the spirit of the granary. For the next two days, Tola observed the women's ritual of eating only lentils and beans and root vegetables. This ritual would ensure that their harvest would be long-lasting and safe from rodents. Every woman of the village observed this ritual and the family tip-toed in and out of the house while the mother sat by the fire, chanting and worshipping the creator-deity. After it was completed, they would join the others in a good harvest festival when everyone had finished bringing their harvests home.

Namu was fast asleep when his grandmother received her visitor. She clamped her hand to her mouth, careful not to let out any sound in alarm. There were no visions this time, only words repeated over and over again. He did not speak audibly for it was her spirit he was addressing.

Get wisdom
Ignorance breeds fear
Get wisdom
Wisdom births courage
Be not hasty to speak
Words are seeds
Be careful not to speak foolishly
Strengthen the hearts of your young
Your people will need courage
To fight the darkness that is surely coming.

He did not linger after that. A great weariness came over Tola and she slept. In her dream, Sungmo came to her and said, 'Tola, you must strengthen Namumolo's heart. Do not fill him with fearful stories as our people do when they are bringing up their young. Do not teach him to fear the wild animals, or the darkness of night, or the spirits. Don't bring him up the way you are expected to. Pass wisdom and courage to him. That is your duty.'

'Sungmo, wait! Tell me more!' She pleaded but Sungmo faded away and Tola woke with a start. She lay quietly trying to remember everything she had been given. Tola reminded herself that she was a dream-receiver. Dream-receivers could always recollect their dreams with great clarity, down to the last detail. Tola repeated to herself the words Sungmo had given her:

Strengthen Namu's heart. Do not teach him fearful stories as our people do when they are bringing up their young. Do not teach him to fear the wild animals, or the darkness of night, or the spirits.

Tola laughed mirthlessly. Parents and grandparents brought up children instilling fear in them. It seemed a perfectly normal thing to do because they themselves had been raised that way. *Don't go out alone, spirits of the night will kill you, don't go to the village pond after dark, strange beings will follow you home, don't wander off, wild animals will surely kill you and eat you up.* When children were small, they were taught to fear the woods, the wild, and the unknown. It was a wonder some of them became great warriors in spite of all the fear they were indoctrinated with from birth. *Don't bring him up the way you are expected to.* Tola perceived the great wisdom there. If she were to strengthen Namu's heart, she could not be sowing fear into his spirit. She would have to consciously stop herself whenever she used scare tactics to prevent him wandering off from her side. A little thrill passed through her heart when she recognised that both Sungmo and the spirit emissary were saying the same thing.

Get wisdom, he had said. *Pass wisdom and courage to him*, Sungmo had repeated. Tola swallowed. *Let these words stay in my heart and guide me. I will do my part*, she prayed.

When it was morning, she went to Chongshen's house, and disclosed her visions and dreams to him. He listened in silence, and at some point, she thought he was getting impatient with her for his face began to darken. Since he did not tell her to stop, she related everything to him and perceived there was no unbelief in his face, but he did request her not to share the visions with anyone else.

'They may not believe you, and worse than that, they may say you are getting a little crazy in your old age. Better not tell anyone,' was his advice. But deep in his heart, he felt jealousy rise and sting at the fact that she was the one chosen to receive the revelations, and not him.

And when he found the opportunity, he remarked to the headman, 'Old lady Tola has been saying some things, but she was quite incoherent. I worry about her, after all she is my cousin, and has no other relative. She has reached the age when people do that, and mumble about dreaming dreams and seeing things.'

Choba looked worried at this information. Tola was an important source of guidance for them both. If she was beginning to lose her focus, that would be a great loss. Perhaps the time was coming for them to lead the village with their own wisdom.

Chapter Nine

Namumolo at fifteen was taller than his grandmother. Tola thought that he resembled his father far more than his mother. When he was deep in thought, it was like seeing the young Topong Nyakba again, the way he knitted his dark brows in concentration, the same determined look on his face that Tola recognised as characteristically Topong Nyakba. He was much stronger than her now, and all the work that they called man's work fell to him. Chopping wood, repairing the house, burning the overgrowth and cutting trees at the jhum field, ploughing the terrace field, and periodically checking that the water sources in the terrace field were not blocked by soil and stones. He had already become very skilled at using his bow and arrows for hunting, and he always carried a spear when he went to the forest.

Namu's initiation into the community of his age-group took place that year. He was quite fearless. At the same time, he was rarely arrogant and always greeted his elders politely. Tola had fulfilled the assignment of strengthening his heart. When he went to the fields, and heard sounds of a tiger prowling about, he would make warrior sounds, and throw challenges to the animal. In the age-group house, they were taught that a tiger could smell fear and hesitation in a hunter, and for this reason young men were instructed not to challenge a tiger if they had the slightest misgiving within them. Most of the young men would never give chase to a tiger if they saw one from afar. Only Namu was known to take off in hot pursuit after man's ancient enemy.

Namumolo was well liked amongst his friends. The young men often went out together, spending nights in the forest, hunting deer and smaller animals. Tola thought they were a little young to be allowed to hunt on their own. But the headman had invited men from the neighbouring village to train their boys to be hunters and good fishermen. Their teachers did their job thoroughly and the boys learned their lessons well. That meant they had knowledge of the places that were to be avoided, and they were well versed about the feeding places that were frequented by wild animals. Choba, the headman, owned a handmade musket he had bought from the Konyaks. His son borrowed it sometimes after receiving strict instructions from his father not to point it at anyone when it was loaded. The rest of the young men hunted with short spears and bows and arrows.

'Befriend the dark,' Namu would tell his friends at such times. 'Make your heart big and stare the night in the face. No, wait, listen, don't laugh. It is good training for your eyes because when you keep staring at the night, your eyes can discern trees from animals, and animals from spirits.'

'And are we to befriend the spirits before they kill us?' Choba's son, Mongba laughed. The other boys guffawed.

'What you don't fear can't hurt you,' was Namu's calm reply.

'You're a strange one, Namu,' Mongba remarked, 'but on a night like this, I'm glad to have you around.' The others continued to laugh at the two of them, although if the truth be told, they all felt uneasy about spending the night in the forest with its strange sounds and sights. It was fine to be in a group, but not one of the boys cared to undertake a hunt singly. Only the older and more experienced hunters did that. The young men couldn't wait for morning to come and end the discomfort of a night hunt. Sitting on a tree branch waiting for game for hours on end quickly took away the excitement of a hunt. It was their good fortune that around midnight, one of them speared a young deer and they spent the rest of the time cleaning and quartering it. At first light, they left for the village with their kill.

Namu's age-group had begun to participate in the many village activities in earnest. They had all learned to play the log-drum and at the big festivals, they eagerly took their places and wasted no time in drumming the festival beat. Elders like Beshang, Choba and Chongshen would initiate the drumming and then they would quickly vacate their seats for the young men, giving up the pleasure they had enjoyed for many years. Quite early on, every child of the village was taught how to recognise the different drum beats, and in particular, the signal for danger. It was the duty of the older men to collect the young boys when they reached the appropriate age, and proceed to teach them how to beat the log drum, because it was such an essential part of their training for life. Even very old men never forgot how the drum was beaten.

'The log-drum is our father,' Choba would remind them. 'It protects us against our enemies and wild animals. When you are out in the fields and you hear the danger signal, no other thought should come to mind save the one to run back to the village and save yourselves or save others. This is why when a log-drum becomes rotten, we waste no time debating how to replace it. We take all the necessary measures well ahead of time and bring a replacement from the forest.'

It was very important to talk in the right manner to the selected tree, using the right words to tell it what they were going to use it for. If they began to cut it without telling the tree their objective, it could cause grievous harm and even bring death to the men. And they would have only their own ignorance to blame for any tragedy. For a tree was a living entity and it would not hesitate to show its anger at any act of disrespect towards it.

The tree was always selected by dreams of the seer. He said that the spirits led him to the appointed tree, and they let him know the exact location of the tree.

When morning came, the seer, accompanied by men from every clan, would locate the tree. He would stand in front of it and address it in a respectful manner. 'Venerable one, we ask you to come with us and be our father. Come and protect our village from our enemies and those who want to see us destroyed. Come and lend us your wisdom. When we use the axe on you, please do not cause harm to the men. Do not fall on anyone and bring about their death. Our only intent is to give you a more noble purpose than that you are fulfilling in the forest. Come and be our voice, call your children home from the dangers that lurk in the forest and beyond. Permit us to use your protection.'

The chosen tree was never cut down in a hurry. In the period of waiting, the seer would have more dreams where the tree would reveal its name, and thereby convey its willingness to be used by the village. Only then would cutting down the tree proceed in earnest. It was the same procedure as was followed with stones that were pulled from the forest and erected in the name of a title-taker. If the stone revealed its name to the title-taker in his dream, it was an indication that dragging the stone home could be performed without any adverse incident. But if the stone declined to reveal its name, it was abandoned immediately no matter how magnificent it was. There was death in the stones that did not want to disclose their names to men. Village history contained enough stories of men dragging stones that were reluctant to reveal their names and meeting their deaths by it.

What was the name of the tree? Often young men foolishly ventured to ask the seer. But the name of a tree was a sacred secret that the seer had to guard with his life. It was not his to impart to others. It was given only by way of granting permission to cut the tree and use it for a further purpose; disclosing its name to another person would bring a curse into the midst of the village. It would lead to men losing their lives when cutting the tree – and that was just the most common consequence. It had also happened that such a tree, when dragged home to the village, failed to protect the village so that both enemy warriors and spirits took off the womenfolk to be slaves or wives or to be new spirits that would haunt their ancestral village. Wise men did not pit their spirits against the spirits of trees. Seers prayed to forget the name of the tree as soon as they woke, because their purpose was fulfilled the minute the tree disclosed its name. It was the same for stones, for a tree-name or a stone-name was not just a name as humans took it to be; it was a part of their spirit essences, and to disclose it to a seer was an act of deep trust. An intimate expression of faith between tree and man. Betraying that trust could not but be met with fatal consequences.

Once the seer had been given the name of the tree, the work of cutting and carving took place shortly after. Making carvings on the log drum was done in the forest. Carefully guarded from the eyes of curious onlookers such as women and children, and even from the eyes of uninitiated men, the work of carving took several weeks to be completed. *Men carve by day, and the spirits come to carve by night.* That was what old men said about the art of carving in the forests. They swore that the sounds of people chanting work songs could be heard through the night when a felled tree was being newly carved. It was the spirit carvers, and no one went to inspect the source when they heard these unusual sounds.

The account of the spirit carvers had their origins in an unusual story. It was the tale of the two brothers who set out to make carvings for their mother who had been deeply wronged by their father. It was a tale repeated by generation to generation. The woman, heavily pregnant with twins, was pushed off a cliff by her husband who accused her of being false to him. The charge was not true; her rivals had poisoned her husband's mind so he would put her away and marry their relative. The woman miraculously survived being pushed off the cliff, and this was taken as a sign of her innocence. But she did not care to return to her husband, and instead, she made her way to another village where a relative took her in, and cared for her when she gave birth to twin sons. The boys resembled their father so closely that everyone who saw them was convinced of their mother's guiltlessness. But the woman would not allow the story of her survival and innocence to be brought before her husband. She was finished with that part of her life.

The boys grew up and were eventually told their mother's story. They were so moved by it that they decided to carve her story on a block of wood to make sure their adoptive village would never forget it. It was a lot of work. The brothers found that the carving was taking much longer than they had estimated so they decided to spend nights in the forest until the work was completed. At such times, their aged mother cooked food and carried it to them. One day, as she approached the site, she heard a multitude of voices. They were chanting work songs as workers were wont to do. 'Oh, their friends must have come to help them,' she said to herself and walked into the clearing. But there were no other people except her two sons.

'Where are your friends?' she asked.

'What friends? It is just us two,' the older son replied.

'But I heard many voices...' It was thoroughly inexplicable and they concluded that the spirits must be at work with them, adding their labours to that of the men's. The carving was so elaborately done that all who saw it marvelled at it. Not only was the story of their mother carved in the wood, there were many other beautiful motifs covering the wooden surface. Neither of the brothers remembered working on those motifs. Stories like this lay behind the practice of treating as sacred tasks the carving of log drums and village gates, and any major carvings. Some drums had carvings of real animals and others had carvings of mythical creatures. Carvers could not give satisfactory explanations about the strange creatures that appeared beside their own work.

But after the most solemn tasks were accomplished, some level of levity would return to the activity of the dragging of the new village log drum. In the great village of Aliba, the men pulling the new log drum, which was colossal, had sung to it, 'Grandfather is going to give you a necklace, *hao-he, hao-he*' as they dragged the drum to the village. The 'necklace' was made of plaited cane and circled the neck of the drum. It was said that the log drum of Aliba could be heard in these villages, Longkhum, Mangmetong and Khensa as well as the Changki area.

Each log-drum was carved with a head, a torso, wings, and a tail. The drumsticks looked like pestles. Smaller villages had smaller log-drums. The bigger the village, the bigger the log-drum. Its duties were announcing public meetings and festivals, warning against enemy attacks, tiger and wild boar attacks and sudden outbreaks of fire. On occasion, it would be played to mourn the dying of the moon or the dying of the sun.

In Namu's village, the village log-drum had been replaced after the attack that took off more than half its occupants. The new seer, Chongshen, had upbraided the old drum for not protecting them.

'Were you sleeping? Did you not hear?' he was heard reprimanding the drum roundly, 'Were you visiting the next village when our enemies came and speared us in our beds? Why did our people perish as though this was a village without a log-drum? Why was there no warning from you? Did you not disclose your name to us when you left your forest home? Or was that not your name at all? Are you our father or are you a stepfather who wishes ill upon his stepchildren?' Those who heard his words were adamant about replacing the old drum, because it was taboo to reproach the log-drum, just as it was taboo to scold or curse one's father or mother. After all, the log-drum was the village deity. Every child was taught to treat it with the respect it deserved. To upbraid it was tantamount to taking an axe to it. The old saying maintaining that a log drum was a living being, taught that a village had to take care not to hurt the feelings of their drum.

The people were fearful that the new seer had surely violated this taboo and if the drum was not replaced, who could tell what further punishment might come to them? No one had ever spoken to the village drum in the manner that Chongshen had done. They always used venerable terms, calling it, 'Our guardian,' 'Our protector,' or 'Father Drum.' Great fear was generated at the foolhardy manner in which the seer had addressed the log drum. *As though it were an equal. As though it had allowed the attack.* Thus, the survivors wasted no time in getting the help of their neighbouring villages to supplant the old drum with a new one.

Chongshen had the task of waiting upon his dreams for many nights to reveal the right tree. Once it was made known, he led the men to the tree and performed the ceremony of addressing the tree using well-chosen words that he had heard the old seer say. Their neighbours sent their carvers to help them make the secret carvings on the body of the drum. The new drum was bigger, and they all agreed that the sound of the new drum carried further than the old drum ever did. The new log drum was protected from the rain and wind by a shelter constructed over it which was to be maintained by the clan living closest to the drum. They would see to it that the thatch on the roof was replaced at the earliest sign of rot, they would replace the bamboo fence around the drum at regular intervals, and their women would be responsible for performing rituals of sprinkling brew on the drum at festivals.

The fate of the old log drum was not enviable: it was abandoned and carelessly cast outside the village gate as it was not to be used for firewood. There it lay, discarded and exposed to the elements and by the time Namu became a teenager the main body of it had rotted. The village children were not allowed to play near it or climb on its surface. It was taboo to beat the discarded drum. Any incidence of people beating the old drum in the middle of the night was dismissed as spirit drumming. Such goings on were, as a rule, never investigated, because the spirits would get angry and blind those who ventured near. If the headman and the seer suspected drunks and hormone-filled young men of breaking the taboo, they agreed it was not worth sending men to examine, as the spirits would themselves mete out justice for taboo violators.

On the nights before a festival, the drum would be beaten in a befitting manner. It would begin with slow overtures designed to gather the people together and the rhythm would pick up from then on. During the festival days, the men said the log-drum begged to be beaten. They said it was like an old woman who knew each and every one of the festival dances, and would begin to tap her feet as soon as the first drum beat sounded. It was that eager to be played. The hard wood responded resiliently, the rhythm flowed out of its crevices, and the wide mouth emitted more sounds than the men were capable of producing with their pestles. 'The spirits join us at festivals,' the men would insist, 'we can hear them playing beats that we have never tried before because they are too fast for human hands to produce!' Was it any wonder that the village people forgot their workdays and circled the drummers, tapping their feet and swaying to the drum beats? The drum of the festival called people away from their fields; it was just as well that festival time was begun after all field work was completed. No one went to the fields during festival season; with the harvesting having been taken care of, people looked forward to the season of feasting. Throughout the winter months, they allowed the fields to lie fallow, and they occupied themselves with hunting of wildlife and gathering herbs and foraging in the forest for food.

'Namu!' Tola's voice reached across the square where Namu was sitting with his mates.

'Why is your mother so much older than any of our mothers?' It was Bumo, the youngest in their age-group.

Namu smiled. He had answered this question before from other friends of his.

'She is my *Abi nyu*, my grandmother,' he replied. 'But she is also my mother, and she is my father. I never knew my parents because they were killed when I was a baby. She was the one who brought me up.'

Bumo looked apologetic for having asked the question so insensitively. The group broke up and each boy went to his own home.

Back in the house, Tola served him food before she got her own food. For all her years, Tola was still active. She went to the fields every day, even though Namu insisted that she should stay at home. He wouldn't allow her to continue with the hard work of ploughing, and they began to make a practice of hiring workers to help them at the most difficult labour of a farmer's life. She insisted on doing her part, a little sowing here, a little transplanting in the next month so that she could daily feel that she was still contributing her share of bringing food home. Her hair was completely grey now, and she was much slower at everything. She took longer to finish cooking, and it was becoming a struggle to fetch water for their home. Yet she would not hear of Namu fetching water. 'It's not a man's job. You will not do it as long as I am alive,' she had stated firmly.

'Fine, fine. Just remember you don't have to fill up the pitcher to the brim,' he replied. Namu took to bathing and washing his clothes at the water source. They were like that with each other because he knew she would try to fill up water for his bath and get very tired from so doing.

When their evening meals were done, and they were sitting by the fire, she would recollect something about Namu's father and begin to narrate it. Namu would bid her to tell him more, but after some time, she would say she had exhausted her memory. She rarely cried now over the son and daughter-in-law whose lives had been cut so tragically short. There were more important things to focus on, and she felt the burden of all the wisdom she had to impart to her grandson. She had resolved to stop looking back at the past; Namu was the future and she would play her part in shaping that future.

Over the years Tola had begun to unravel her dreams and visions to Namu. It was part of the reality she belonged to, the reality she always wanted him to embrace. On his part, he listened without interrupting her; he had never had any reason to doubt what she shared with him. He trusted his grandmother implicitly. But he had not experienced anything of the spirit world yet. Perhaps he would encounter it when he grew a little older. After all, the blood of seers ran in his veins as well.

One evening she broached the subject of getting him a wife. Namu had now entered his twenties. Most of his friends had married or were about to marry.

The name she mentioned was Thongdi, the granddaughter of Beshang, the widower.

'She's not from our age-group.' Namu hoped he had made it sound like a protest.

'No, but she is old enough to marry.'

'I don't think she even knows me.' He was still protesting but more feebly now.

'Everyone knows everyone else in the village. That's how we get to know if a young woman will make a good wife or not.' In his mind's eye, Namu pictured the modest young woman who had greeted him with a shy smile when he passed her in the village square. She had the clear complexion of the women of her clan, and was known to be a hard worker. Thongdi was polite and well brought up; both young and old praised her. The more Namu thought about it, the more the idea of courting her appealed to him.

'You will take an offer yourself? Or will you ask Uncle Chongshen?' Namu asked.

'No need to disturb Chongshen. He is the seer. That places him above all other ordinary tasks that the family performs. I will go myself.'

Thongdi's people were very happy to receive the proposal. Namu was well liked in their village. He was known as a young man respectful to older people and regarded well among his peers, and admired by the groups younger to his age-group. Thongdi's mother called her daughter a fortunate young woman. After the proposal was made, the mother dreamed of her cows birthing very healthy calves. In another dream, the trees on her land grew taller than the trees on her neighbour's land. All these were good dreams for a successful union, and Thongdi's parents made up their minds quite easily. The rituals for marriage proceeded very smoothly. Thongdi's grandparents were title-takers and they insisted on providing cattle for the wedding feast.

After some weeks of preparation, Namu's bride was brought home following the harvest festival. At Tola's insistence he had built another house on their land, and the newlyweds began their life together in the new house. If the wedding plans were agreed upon, it was quite acceptable for a groom to build a new house before the marriage took place. Tola did not want the young bride to find her interfering in their lives. She knew that sharing a house with a strange old woman would be intimidating enough to any young woman. They would have separate hearths and they would share meals together when they wanted to, not because they had to. It was a good arrangement. The young Thongdi was happy to have her own house, but she insisted on helping Tola with some of the chores in her home. Ever so often, she cooked meals for the three of them.

Chapter Ten

At the next festival season, Beshang the widower died. He had been ailing for a long time, and one night when a great storm raged through the countryside, uprooting young trees and threatening to blow down houses, he breathed his last. The villagers said the storm had come to take him, because as soon as Beshang died, it left as suddenly as it had come. At his funeral, he was given the honour due to the oldest member of the village and mourned as befitted the old warrior and carrier of stories. The log drum was beaten in a slow, mournful manner so that neighbouring villages would thus be informed that an important member of the village had passed away. If anyone wanted to attend the funeral, they would be able to come on hearing the message. For many people who had relatives or friends living in other villages, this was one way of communicating news of a death.

Thongdi and her parents were deeply grieved at Beshang's death; they mourned their gentle storytelling father and grandfather, and the villagers wept with them when they came to chant his praises. Thongdi helped her mother to wash the body and prepare it. Two elderly women came from the neighbour village and covered him with a body-cloth. One of them was Beshang's cousin Nati. She placed a small bag of seed grains beside his head.

'Go well, elder brother,' the white-haired Nati said in a low voice. 'We will soon follow you.' The funeral rites were performed by his son and grandson.

After Beshang's funeral, a period passed when several of the villagers sighted his spirit and the spirit of his wife outside his house. It frightened his neighbours and there was talk of pulling down the old widower's house. But the headman would not allow that to happen. 'Has anyone been harmed? Have the spirits proved themselves dangerous to any member of the village? No? Then no one has the right to declare they may not come and go as they please in what was their property before they turned spirit. His house will not be taken down. Who knows if they have come to bless us?' Some more weeks went by, and there were no further reports of spirit sightings. The fear died down as well, and talk ceased on the subject.

Tola no longer went to the fields. She used a cane to help her move about. Her hearing was still good, although the same could not be said about her sight. Namu's wife Thongdi was pregnant with their first child. It was early days yet, but they had begun to think of names already. Thongdi had confided to Tola that she wanted lots of children. It warmed Tola's heart. The village had grown to twenty households again and showed no signs of stopping there. Tola sometimes thought about the visions she had had so many years ago. It seemed as though all of that had happened in another lifetime. She was in her nineties now, and she often wondered if the things revealed to her would come to pass before she left for the afterlife. She reminded Namu about them whenever they were together. At least someone should know when it happened and what to do about it, although she wasn't quite sure what was to be done. But she had abided by the admonition to strengthen Namu's heart. He was young but wise in the way he received the things of the spirit from his grandmother. Not like some of his friends who scoffed at spirit things and called him an old woman when he tried to speak about them.

But the story of the great darkness was a story told in other villages as well. It was told by travellers stopping for the night in villages along the way. When Choba's father Chingmak was the headman, he had hosted travellers at different times and some of the men talked about it with conviction. They narrated their versions of the prophecy that a time was coming when the world would be covered in darkness, and each village had to be prepared to combat it in their own way. The travellers said their seers had warned them about it, which was why no sensible traveller would spend the night in the forest if he could help it. He would always find a village and take shelter for the night. Some people even thought it was an event that had happened a very long time ago. But these were in the minority and the main narrative was that it was yet to come.

Yet the day it came to them, it caught everyone unawares, because no one was prepared for the extent of the darkness and how completely it would transform what they had always taken for granted. When they heard the drums there had been some hesitation among the people out in the fields. Many of them were hearing the rhythm beaten as a warning for the first time outside the village territory.

It was the older ones who recognised the urgency in the warning signal and they were the ones who shouted at the others to leave everything and run back to the safety of the village. They had called across the fields to those who might not be aware of the signal. Later, they would find out what was wrong. But right now, they needed to outrun the drums.

Namu's pregnant wife was pulled away by her elderly neighbour. Her basket on her back, she joined the crowd of frightened people who were trying to obey the summons of the drums. Even as she ran, she saw how dark it had become. At the turning she glanced behind her and was shocked at the black wall that had fallen and separated them from the fields. It was not possible to see beyond it. It terrified her, and she ran harder than ever trying to put distance between herself and the great blackness. The closest fields were less than an hour's walk from the village. The first batch reached the gate after two hours; they took so long because they could not see their way in the darkness and they had to be led back by the hunters.

Choba was standing guard at the village gate. He was accompanied by the seer, both of them looking very grim. Chongshen carried a bamboo torch with him.

'You're safe now,' he called out to the disorderly lot that were straggling in. They were out of breath and could barely greet him. 'Go home and rest. We'll find out what is wrong.' He continued to speak comfortingly to them as they filed into the open gate. Men stumbled in carrying children on their backs followed by women clinging to their baskets, old women pulled along by their sons, and old men falteringly following the crowd. The younger members came last because the young men had remembered that at times such as these, they should be strong hearted and bring up the rear after making sure weaker members had been rescued. They had their spears out and looked ready for any eventuality, but deep inside they all knew that their spears were no weapon against this enemy. It was more unnerving than being chased by an army of enemy warriors. When they entered the village, the sound of the drums was deafening.

'Do you think they have all come back?' Chongshen asked Choba anxiously.

'We will take a head count and find out. Stop the drums now and set guards at the gate. We will need to close the gate soon if this persists.'

Chongshen ran to the shed where the log drum was kept. Signalling to the men to stop, he sent Namu and Mongba to do a head count of each house. The men returned after checking all the houses, and gave their report. Two families whose fields were the furthest had not returned. All the others had come back safely.

What was to be done? Choba requested the drummers to play on further in the hope that the missing families would hear it and try to come home. But the drumming was in vain. They never came. The drummers were exhausted when the headman finally said they could stop. The last drum notes echoed back from the valley and then everything fell silent.

'*Heii! Weii*! We are shutting the gate now!' The headman's voice carried through the darkness. 'We have waited for many hours for all our people to come back to the village, but it is no longer safe to keep the gate open. The fierce animals are hungry. We hear them baying. We cannot sacrifice the safety of the many for the sake of the few. In the morning, the men will go and look for the missing ones. *Heii! Weii*! May no evil come to our people!'

This was normal practice that every villager was familiar with. After nightfall, the big wooden gate was closed against enemy warriors, wild animals and spirits. Night always brought its own set of dangers. One year they had been troubled by packs of wild dogs that dragged off chickens and piglets. The men were ready the following nights with firebrands and spears, and they killed the whole pack, hunting down the ones that had run off. Tigers and bears kept to the woods, but that was no guarantee they would not come to the village to take off cattle. If they were wounded and could not hunt for food, they preyed on the slow-moving village cows. The shutting of the gate ensured the safety of the village every night.

The drummers returned to their homes and families. Namu found his house empty because Thongdi had gone directly to Tola's house where they were talking about the calamitous happening. The only light in the room was from the fireplace. Tola was sitting up in her bed with Thongdi seated beside her, the dying fire lending an eerie glow to the room. Thongdi had her arms around the old woman's shoulders. Tola could not stop trembling. When Namu entered, his grandmother looked up at him.

'Namu!' Tola cried. 'It has come! Tiger has eaten the sun!'

'Yes Grandmother. You were right. It's terrible. Two families have not come back from the fields. I don't know what we are going to do.'

'If they stay in their huts, they may be safe, but no one can tell what will happen now,' Tola answered.

'Grandmother, do you know how long this will last? You must tell us all that you know.'

'Has the seer said anything yet?'

'No. Uncle Chongshen was busy helping the headman at the gate. We did a head count and that is how we found out about the missing families. Their houses were bolted from outside and no one could recollect seeing them when running back from the fields. The headman said the men would have to go look for them in the morning.'

'Morning may not come, Namu.' Tola's voice sounded ominous, but she was only stating what she knew. 'It was a long period of darkness that I saw, many days, many, many days.'

'What shall we do? Tell us what to do, Grandmother.' Tola looked away from her grandson to peer into the fire. After some moments she turned to the young people and when she spoke, her voice was calm and emphatic.

'I am not the seer. It is his job to tell us what to do. But on our part, we will stay brave. That is our weapon. Stay courageous and wise. Do nothing foolish. It was not for nothing that the spirit emissary repeatedly gave those words: Courage. Wisdom. Namu, don't be in a hurry to do anything. The wrong rituals can push us into further trouble.'

Namu saw something of the spirit of the old days in his grandmother when she spoke in that manner. Of late, she had become quite frail and forgetful and he didn't like leaving her alone when they went to the fields. Now he could see she had found her fighting spirit back. She was already telling him what to do even while protesting that it was not her job to be seer. In spite of the horror of the situation, Namu felt a little hope revive in his heart. The old Tola had come back. How much could she remember? Would it be enough to save them all?

'I am not afraid, Grandmother,' Namu assured her. 'And I will be careful.'

'Good,' Tola replied. 'This fight will not be won without some suffering, but we were not unaware of it. The worst thing is if a village is unprepared when an attack comes – if the spirits had not given any warning beforehand, it means it is to be the death of the village. But if the spirits have been giving us prior warning, it means the thing will not kill us. We are destined to survive it.'

Thongdi quickly made some food and they ate in silence and the meal seemed to take some of their fatigue away.

Not every household had the clarity of Tola's family. For the most, people were filled with great trepidation at the all-enveloping darkness. When they thought of their neighbours who had not managed to come back, their hearts felt as though they would burst from despair. It was worse than death, it was a living death, to be so afraid and unable to do anything about it.

Chapter Eleven

There was no respite from the darkness. People stayed up and watched and waited. But the thick blackness had completely covered the land. They looked skyward to see if the moon and the stars had come out but it was as though a thick mantle had been drawn across the face of the sky. It was darker than a moonless night.

It was a darkness that was different from anything they had ever experienced. It was different from the half-moon nights when fathers would hoist their toddlers on their backs and take them outside to look at the moon. On those nights, fathers told their young children the story of a man called Ningtanger who had thrown cow-dung at the moon because the moon had killed his mother and he was so angry that he did the first thing that came to mind: he threw dung at the moon and it stayed on the moon's face, and they would see the dung-covered face of the moon in a few days. No, it was completely different from that kind of night sky. It was different from those moonless nights when young men's hearts warmed to the thought of congregating at the dormitory to listen to stories of hunts their seniors had gone on, and tales of the battles the village had won. It was nothing like the nights when teenage girls sat up singing songs of love and courtship, dreaming of the day they would become young wives. There was no romance or magic to this dark time, except perhaps its own baneful magic. This blackness had eclipsed anything resembling light, man-made or natural. It drove them to despair and robbed them of all energy.

It left them crushed and defeated and the exhaustion wore them down into a dreamless sleep, from which they woke hoping to find that it was morning. But there was no morning, no light, no nothing. There was utter confusion. The headman quickly realised that if this continued, there would be no means of telling one day from another. He also feared this could go on for a very long time. They must have some way of telling time. The seer was the person responsible for calculating the lunar calendar and announcing the festival days or *genna* days. But when it was not possible to see the moon and the stars, how would he do that? How to tell day from night when it was perpetually night? How to tell time?

People shut their doors and spoke in whispers to each other. It stayed pitch-black outside. The roosters had not crowed. Namu knew it must be morning because he had woken up wanting to urinate. Making his way to the fireplace, he poked at the glowing firebrand and piled bamboo shavings atop it. He put a couple of pieces of wood on the fire and got it going before he cautiously opened the door. He could not see anything in front of him. Turning back, he grabbed a long-handled knife before opening the door a little wider. He squeezed out of the opening sideways, and made his way to the outhouse. It was eerie to be standing outside. The village wall was about eight feet high. Beyond it were fields and dense forest. When Namu climbed up to the roof and looked at the forest, he could see pin-points of light. The lights moved swiftly to and fro, and he suspected it was an animal, no human could move that fast. He scrambled down and ran back inside and secured the door against whatever was lurking outside.

Lying back in bed, he heard faint noises. It was the village waking up, but it was nothing like on the other days. Every sound was subdued. No children cried, no one spoke loudly, and it seemed as though the darkness was being perpetuated by the fearful silence of the people. Not one soul wanted to risk going out of their homes to find out if anything had changed in the course of the night.

As the day wore on, the one thing that occurred with a fair amount of regularity was hunger. The people felt hungry at periodic intervals. The headman Choba realised that mealtimes could probably be used to tell time. Excitedly he began to put notches on the inner beam of his house after the third meal of the day, the third meal being equivalent to the evening meal. They felt quite sleepy soon after finishing the third meal and followed it up with a long sleep. The first meal after the long sleep would then approximate as the morning meal, and for Choba that signalled the beginning of a new day. After making this discovery, Choba went out of his house on the second day. He carried his father's old gong and beat on it a few times before making his announcement. The gong echoed round the village, and made people attentive. Choba shouted,

'*Heii! Weii*! It is the second day of the darkness. Keep your hearts alert!'

Making notches after each long sleep, and beating the gong to announce a new day was the best that he could do seeing that they could no longer rely on the roosters to crow at first light.

It reminded him of the story of the village of Mvüphri where the chief and seven of his best warriors went on a journey they were advised not to make. Though the seer had warned that that if they went out of the village gate, there would be no guarantee of protection, the chief remained thick-eared and obdurate. He had insisted that the business could not be put off any longer. The seven men volunteered to go with him. They would not relent to the pleas of their wives. 'How can I lift my head up if I let him go to meet his fate alone? It is for such a day that I am a warrior. One day my son will understand and be proud of me. Better a dead warrior for a father than a weak-hearted coward who is still living. There is no dignity in such a life and why should you want to be the wife of such a man?' They made their farewells full knowing this could be the last time they saw their loved ones. Had there been a little touch of arrogance to them? Could anyone fault them if they had had a bit of faith in themselves? More than the seer seemed to have?

But a seer is not a seer for nothing, and spirits can deceive men into thinking they will be passed over only so they can have the pleasure of taking them down at their most vulnerable. The eight men were never heard of again. The village found out that something had gone horribly wrong when the roosters refused to crow. Rooster after rooster failed to crow at daybreak. It was not long after that the people came to consult the seer. He knew that the men had gone to their deaths, but he said nothing because he wanted to confirm it thoroughly; besides, these signs were good for the people to know. It would build up their faith in the supernatural. So, he gave no immediate answer to their many questions. After a few more days, when the whole village was agog with the abnormal situation of roosters refusing to crow, they came to the seer again, and this time he explained the revelation that had been neglected by the warriors and the chief. That was how the people came to know that the chief and the seven had met with unnatural deaths. No other men's lives would be risked to search for their bodies. The seer had stopped them with the saying: *When the spirits kill a man, they also bury the man. No one can find the burial places chosen by the spirits.* The funeral rites of the men were arranged after this confirmation of their deaths, and the story spread to neighbouring villages to be recounted as a deterrent against disbelief.

An old woman of Mvüphri had remarked, 'If a man's time has come, there is no force that can stop him from going out and meeting his death. That is what has happened to these men. No ritual is sufficient to circumvent the hour of death. Had they stayed at home, who knew if death would not have come for them if it was their time. Men have been known to fall down in their own courtyards and die there.'

'But what about the stories of men who defied their death-destinies and lived?' the young ones had asked. The reply was, 'There were a few such men, but their numbers were so few that their stories have passed into legend. And their deaths were averted only for a number of years; the truth is they all died eventually, of sickness or old age. Avoiding death is not something that an ordinary person can aspire to. No one can make a bargain with death.'

Tola's village had entered the third day of darkness. Chongshen, the seer, sat chanting by the fire, hoping to invoke guardian spirits that could give him some clues as to what rituals he should perform. But the long hours of chanting yielded no answers. He had not forgotten about Tola's visions. But deep inside, he desired a personal revelation that he could own and proudly use to play his role in saving the village. He was their seer after all, was he not? For this very reason, his house lay adjoining the headman's house. They were the two most important men in the village.

When the headman came to him, he had no answers.

'Perhaps someone has committed a grave taboo,' was the best answer he could come up with. 'Let us question all of them minutely: perhaps someone has moved an ancient boundary marker, or spat on a spirit-stone, or done something far worse.'

The headman agreed to that. They were both aware that people might lie. How to best go about it? They would promise secrecy, and not use the threat of public censure. They would approach them as elders approach a child, coaxing the truth out of young minds by persuading them that a confession was something that would end in a reward, not punishment.

Going from house to house, they sat with the frightened villagers in their homes and tried to sound reassuring.

'Taboos are made for our protection. If a taboo is violated, it is not the end. The consequences of a taboo violation can be undone with the right rituals of propitiation. Have we not seen many of our members healed from sicknesses that befell them when they wandered into places that are forbidden? Have we not offered enough chicken sacrifices to keep the spirits happy? If any of you have committed a taboo, knowingly or unknowingly, try to remember it. We will all work together to undo it and save our village from the curse of the great darkness. Who knows we may be able to save other villages as well by our actions!'

It was a fruitless endeavour. With as much conviction as they could muster, Choba and Chongshen promised the people they would do all they could to protect the village. In every house that they entered, the people looked anxious and confused, and there was nothing they could say or do to alter that before they left. The two men asked inane questions on whether the villagers had enough food stocks. It was the middle of the year. Every household, even the poorest of all, still had food grains from the year before. Warning people not to be wandering about in the dark, they went back to Choba's house. The village gate would remain closed so long as the dark time persisted.

'See if you will be shown anything in your dreams,' Choba whispered as they parted.

On the fourth day, Chongshen came to Choba.

'Perhaps I should travel to the seer at Mvüphri mountain. He might be able to tell me what to do,' Chongshen suggested.

'I cannot allow you to do that. No seer leaves the borders of the village. If he does, he takes away the virtue of the village with him, have you forgotten? Not to speak of the danger of you being killed on the way! Chongshen, I do not give you permission to go to Mvüphri.'

'But if this goes on for a long time, and we do nothing about it, we will still die. In fact, we may all die. Isn't it better to risk one life rather than risk all?'

Choba was not convinced. 'If someone has to travel to find answers, it should be me or a warrior, not you.'

'The people need you here. You are the headman. More than anyone else, they need you here to guide them. They have so much fear it is almost tangible.'

It took about two days to finally convince Choba that Chongshen could make a journey without endangering the virtue of the village. If someone was willing to be seer in his place, he could travel as an ordinary citizen.

'Namu can be seer in my absence,' Chongshen suggested.

'Namu! He is too young. What would he know?' Choba protested.

'Well, he is the great-grandson of a seer, and Tola is there to teach him what he does not know.' That was a possibility that Choba had not thought of.

But Namu was very hesitant when they approached him. 'If you really need a person from the line of seers, why not take Grandmother?'

'Only a male can be seer,' was the reply he got. Very reluctantly, Namu agreed to the arrangement. He would be confined to the village until Chongshen returned and in his absence, he would have to perform sanctification rituals for the village.

'Grandmother, it is not right. Tell me what to do,' he begged the old woman.

'Namu, it is right. You must pray for wisdom as you already have courage.'

Chongshen left immediately for the mountain. Two men went with him, lighting their way with wormwood torches. But they did not get very far. Spirits attacked them at the second field. Chongshen raised his spear and shouted authoritatively at them, but he was no longer seer. He was travelling as an ordinary person without any protection. A spirit flew at him, almost blinding him. Pain seared his eyes and he struggled to keep standing. His two companions were petrified.

'Come on!' he shouted at them, trying to recover his composure. To turn back now was death. All they could do for the time being was to press on and hope that their doggedness would deceive the spirits into thinking they were immune to their attacks. With luck, they might still carry out their mission.

Tersely Chongshen ordered the two men to follow him as he pressed into the crowd of thronging spirits and marched through them. His bluff seemed to work as the ones at the back gave way having seen that the ones in front did nothing to detain them.

Mount Mvüphri was not very far from their village. They used their torches sparingly, burning only one at a time until they came to the foot of the mountain. Their hearts lifted when they reached the rocky borders of Mvüphri, for they knew no spirit would dare pursue them beyond its borders.

Mvüphri was known for its integrity. Its people were forthright and devoid of guile. Their uprightness protected them from spirits like an impregnable shield. Consequently, they had become one of the most powerful villages for many miles around. Mvüphri was also the only village older than Namu's village, *Shumang Laangnyu Sang*.

'What foolhardiness to travel here!' The seer of Mvüphri was very angry. 'Have you really exhausted the resources of your village that you had to risk life and limb and come to me?'

Chongshen was quite taken aback by the rebuke from the seer of Mvüphri. He had expected a warm welcome. As a fellow-seer, he had expected sympathy in his situation and an offer of help. Instead, the seer of Mvüphri was positively castigating him in front of the two men with him. How could he face his villagers when the men reported on his treatment at Mvüphri?

'We have exhausted our resources,' Chongshen replied, trying to keep the irritation from his voice. Didn't this old man know how much they had risked to get here? Couldn't he be more civil? 'None of the villagers can remember committing a taboo that could have resulted in this curse of darkness.'

The areas around Mvüphri were shrouded in darkness too. Chongshen's words fell on deaf ears. The old seer's eyes smouldered.

'We have come here seeking you because everyone knows you are a much more powerful seer than I ever will be.' Chongshen hoped these words would placate the seer of Mvüphri. His expression had certainly changed. It had turned from anger to incredulity. His long, gray hair shook as he spluttered,

'Do you really not know you have an equally powerful seer in the village? One maybe even more powerful than I?'

Chongshen was stupefied. For once, he had no words. The seer of Mvüphri saw it at once.

'You fool! You have let your jealousy thoroughly blind you to the tremendous help you could have gotten from her. Yes! I mean Tola! You should have gone to her. You are seer only of the calendar and crops and festivals. But she is the seer of men's destinies! Did she not bring you her visions and dreams? Did you not tell her to tell no one about it? Do you deny that?'

'No, no, I didn't mean it like that... it was so long ago... she is an old woman and you know how old women are... in any case, there have never been female seers in the history of my village.'

Chongshen knew how feeble his excuses sounded. The men who had come with him hung their heads and avoided meeting his eyes. This public upbraiding was the last thing any of them had expected!

'No women seers?' the seer of Mvüphri positively snorted. 'Beyond this mountain there are great female seers who are much more powerful than male seers. My own mother was seer before me. Yes, didn't anyone tell you? For a long time, ignorant men have said, 'Old women and their tales!' and laughed at them and laughed the truth of those tales away. Disbelief kills miracles. Disbelief throttles the truth, but not for long. It always comes out, if not in this age, then in the next. Your great rankling jealousy of her will not stop her visions from coming true.'

Chongshen was visibly moved. He hid his face in his hands and lowered his head. Every word the seer said was true. His jealousy of Tola had festered for many years because he had never seen any visions in his long career as seer. He had had a few dreams which he made much of and presented to the village as though the creator-deity had himself spoken to him. And it was not so long ago that he had insinuated to Choba that Tola was getting so old she was beginning to speak incoherently. In seemingly innocuous ways, he had suggested that the oldest member of the village was no longer to be trusted to give sound advice. Choba, who knew no better, and trusted in the seer's judgment, believed him unquestioningly. After all he was seer. Shame and disgust now swept over him. The two men who came with him had heard everything. They would carry the stories back and the whole village would get to know his whole life had been a sham. The men still stood there in embarrassed silence, looking away from the two seers. Chongshen was shame-stricken by each revelation. What was worse than that was the probability that his disgraceful behaviour had possibly activated the curse. He had to find out.

'The darkness – have I, have I caused it with my conduct?'

The seer of Mvüphri shook his head. 'No. This is a spirit thing. A terrible thing has happened in the spirit world. *The sacred has been profaned.* It is beyond us. But all creation will suffer the effects of the profanity and maybe creation will have a hand in restoring the light again.'

Chapter Twelve

The sacred has been profaned.

Chongshen had no idea what the seer of Mvüphri meant by that. He was coming to terms with the fact that his spiritual knowledge was so scanty that his mind could not grasp an iota of what went on in the spiritual world.

'Then there is nothing to do but wait, is there?' Chongshen asked.

'Waiting is futile if it is just waiting. Waiting must be accompanied by an attitude of seeking and receiving wisdom. Waiting is pointless if it is inactive.'

'How does one do that? How to wait… actively?' Chongshen asked with some hesitation.

'One starts with ridding oneself of all that has been allowed to enter and pollute the mind. By an active cleansing of our thoughts. Hatred and enmity, envy, murderous and lustful thoughts, all such thoughts must be discovered and uprooted. Pride and self-interest too. *One cannot receive when one is full.* And that is not all. Casting out fears, embracing trust – that naturally becomes the next step.'

The men were silent, each one concentrating on the seer's words.

'Waiting is not just for seers. The whole community must participate. Pray that your village will be enlightened with that teaching.'

Silence fell over the room as each man struggled with his thoughts. After some time, Chongshen spoke. 'Well, we should rest a bit and be heading back. They will be worried about us.'

'Go back? Man, are you quite mad? You can deceive the spirits once. But a second time is very unlikely. If you try to return, you will surely be killed. Listen, listen! can you not hear the dirges they are already singing over you?'

The men pricked up their ears but could hear nothing. The seer's eyes dug into theirs as he compelled them to keep listening.

The thin voices chanting dirges made the hair on their heads stiffen in deep dread. The voices were singing funeral dirges, female voices calling their names one by one. The words were not audible, but they easily recognised the melody of the dirge, and they heard their names punctuating the death chant repeatedly. They recalled that men who were destined to die shortly would receive death chants that no one else could hear. Tears streamed down the first man's face. 'I don't want to die,' he blubbered. 'I love my children.'

They were all quite unmanned by the singing. Even Chongshen was visibly moved.

'Stay here. Your families will worry, indeed they will. But think how much happier they would be if you returned safely to them after the period of waiting is over. We will share our food with you. Don't protest, it is not luxurious, but it is nutritious and we have more than enough for guests. My house is made for receiving guests. We have more rooms than we ever use. They are deliberately built for situations like these.'

The men had many questions but dared not ask their grim host. Thankfully, his family members intervened by leading them to the kitchen where two of the many fireplaces were still burning. His wife served them food and made beds ready for them. Whenever thoughts of home and family crept into their minds, they trained themselves to think on their glad reunion in the future, and not of the anxiety they would be causing their loved ones. This village was none other than the village of Mvüphri whose former chief had set out with his best warriors unheeding of the advice of his seer. They all knew the story of how the men had never returned and the roosters had stopped crowing for several days. It made the three men realise how fatal it was to override a seer's injunctions. All of them were aware how powerful the seer of this village was, and they did not doubt they would be safe where they were. They could only pray for the same protection over their loved ones at home.

Back in the village, Choba and Namu were worried about what to tell the families of the three men when they did not return. There were tears. There were questions. There were tears again. And finally, there was resignation in the women's faces. Until news of their deaths came in one way or other, they would go on with their lives as though their husbands had gone on a long journey and would return one day. They would live with hope until it was snuffed out.

With Chongshen gone, Namu was introduced as the seer of the village. Choba talked to him as though he were the spiritual guardian of the village. Like an equal. In reality, Namu was the same age as Choba's son, Mongba. He had always addressed Choba as uncle and continued to do so. Namu felt very nervous about the new role he was called upon to play, and he fervently prayed for the darkness to end soon. If not for the fact that his grandmother would help him, he would have done anything to avoid being seer.

The dark time had now entered the twelfth day. It was not the sort of darkness that your eyes got accustomed to when you stood in it for a time. That darkness allowed you to make out shapes in the dark so you could distinguish between houses and trees, and a shape that looked ghostly and menacing would turn out to be a pestle leaning against the wall or a water pitcher placed upside down. This darkness was so thick you could not see your hand in front of you. It hit you the moment you went out the door, like someone had thrown a blanket over your head.

People used their wormwood torches to get from house to house. But no one had thought to keep a good supply of wormwood, and they had to be careful not to use them up. Choba and Namu tried to visit each house at least once a day to encourage people and make sure they had food in their homes.

'What does the seer say?' they would all ask. 'Is there something we should be doing?' These were the questions they all wanted answered. By now the people had accepted that Namu was the new seer and they were expecting him to declare a fast or a series of *genna-days*, any of the ceremonies wherein the whole village could take part. Namu simply smiled and replied that he would let them know if such a need arose.

Tola had not received any more dreams or visitations. They were all disappointed. She would lie in bed sleepless wondering if she had imagined it all. However, one night, not long after Namu had become seer, she dreamed of the spirit emissary.

'Cleanse yourself Tola.' He spoke as though she should know what he was referring to. This time Tola was not restrained from speaking.

'Cleanse myself of what?' Tola asked. 'I am ready to do so, but I must know what to do.'

'You have doubted. You have thought that you had imagined the visions and dreams. Rid yourself completely of all disbelief. Namu needs you now more than ever.' Realisation came to Tola immediately. Her visitor looked sterner than ever as he stood stiffly in front of her, as though waiting for his information to sink in. She looked at him expecting more revelations but there was nothing more. The spirit emissary's face was like a mask; he looked cold and aloof as though conveying that his time was wasted on people who doubted him. He left abruptly after that.

Tola repented instantly. She strengthened herself by recollecting every visitation she had been given in the past. She repeated to herself the words she had been given for Namu. She would never doubt again.

After that the visions returned. Tola called Namu to tell him the same truths that the Seer of Mvüphri had pronounced. It is a spirit thing. *The sacred has been profaned. Something so dreadful has taken place in the spirit world, and therefore the human world is reeling from its disorder. There is no taboo we can perform to undo it. Everyone must stay within the village and avoid actions that lack wisdom. Let people learn to wait actively, and expectantly. The creator-deity will provide deliverance in the midst of obedience, but rebellion will end in destruction.*

Namu shared all these revelations with the rest of the village. Every member sought to abide by his instructions.

Then on, Tola had visions every night, each one more appalling than the first. She would call for Namu in a loud voice and he would come running because he was a very light sleeper.

'The village is not safe anymore,' she cried out one night.

'What do you mean, Grandmother? I thought we were safe so long as we stayed within the walls. The gate has not been opened all this time after the seer left.'

'It is not safe within the walls now. Don't allow people to leave their houses. If they step outside, they could be attacked and killed,' she said with tears. In her visions, the areas outside people's homes were infested with spear-carrying spirits who were waiting to kill people the minute they left the safety of their homes. Within the village, the headman had not restricted the movement of people. They left their houses for short periods to enquire after elderly relatives and also find out if their neighbours had some extra information. Now his grandmother was asking all that to be stopped.

'Get the headman to announce that no one is to come out of their house now.'

The village of twenty households, housing nearly fifty people with very different personalities, was not easy to keep bridled. People complained.

'How can they stop us visiting each other?'

'We should get the old seer back.'

'This one does not know anything.'

'He is too young.'

'It's gone to his head.' That was what some of them said. They questioned why they should obey anything the young one said. Namu despaired of making any headway with the people.

But one evening, a dirge was heard from one of the houses. A solitary woman's voice singing a dirge for her husband. That was how the others found out that someone had died at the far end of the village. Possibly he had disobeyed the seer and gone out of his house. They listened carefully to the words of the dirge. She sang his praises and sang her loss and ended with the words, *Food for the spirits*. The woman sang for a long time. She repeated this phrase again and again. Bleak though it was, dirge singing became the new form of communication in the dark time.

'It sounds like it was a spirit kill,' Namu said to his wife and grandmother. The two of them had moved into Tola's house after the instructions for people to stay within their homes were given. Tola's house was bigger, and with all of them under one roof, Namu felt he could look after his family better. He had brought wood from their house and made sure the fire was kept burning at all times, so the kitchen area was always lit.

'What about the body, Grandmother?' Namu asked. All that Tola knew of a spirit kill was that the spirits would take the body with them. There was no question of recovery or possibility of burial, and this was what she told them.

'No one must go out,' Thongdi said. 'If they do, they are responsible for anything that happens to them. Grandfather taught us about these things. He said that heeding the taboos ultimately becomes a matter of life and death. The present time is the strongest test of that.'

Thongdi's words made Namu remember why his grandmother chose her to be his bride. She had grown up listening to the teaching of her parents and grandparents. He was grateful for such a thoughtful mate; their culture never encouraged the open show of affection, so they used loving words with each other instead. From day one of their marriage, Thongdi had taken over caring for Tola, and she did it well.

Two more days passed and the second dirge was heard. It came from the eastern side of the village. This time it was an old woman who lived with her daughter. The deeply melancholic dirge was sung for what seemed like hours on end. The singer sang the praises of the dead woman. She chanted the reason of her death repeating it over and over again until her voice grew lower and sobbing replaced the singing. In the unaffected houses people mourned along with her. Deaths were a community affair.

In normal times, they would have congregated at the house of the dead member, and helped the family to complete the rituals and kept the bereaved family company. Some members would have cooked for the bereaved and others would have sat with the families for many days as they grieved. In the village, no one was allowed to bear their grief alone. But now there was nothing to be done, unless they broke the prohibition and ended up breaking themselves too. Then what good would that do to their community?

Their salvation would come by obeying their leaders and heeding what the seer and the headman said. One of the instructions from the headman was to ask people to dig a deep hole at the back of their houses that they could use as a temporary outhouse. Since every house had a narrow door at the back, and a fence around the house, this was easily done. Even though it was abhorrent to them to have an uncovered outhouse so close to the house, the people recognised that it was necessary in the darktime if they did not want to be exposed to spirit attacks. When normalcy returned, sanctification of the houses would be among the first rituals to be performed.

People had learned to be extremely cautious now not to break any of the taboos in case that somehow led to lengthening the period of darkness. There was another thought on people's minds that they were afraid to voice – were the spirits isolating them from one another so that they could finish them off one by one? The deaths intensified the sense of isolation.

Chapter Thirteen

By the twentieth day of the dark time, four people had been killed. Two young children – one of whom was the infant son of Choba's daughter – had been taken away within two days of each other. It was hard for people to obey the seer's instruction not to be fearful. Namu repeatedly asked everyone to live above their fears and doubts. He said it would be their weapon to fight the darkness. But no heart was inclined to work on that. Of course, they feared the darkness. Of course, they feared the spirits that were killing off their friends and neighbours every week. Of course, they feared the unknown.

There was another thing to be anxious about. Ever since the dark time started there had been no rainfall. It was most strange. In the week before the darkness descended, the grain had been forming on the paddy stalks. This was the season when it would need a lot of water, especially in the terrace fields. If the water drained out, the plants would not survive. One year, a sudden dry period had killed off the rice plants. The young ears of grain that had been looking so promising shrivelled up and turned black. It was good only for cattle fodder. There had been nothing they could do. After that dry period passed, they sowed their fields again, this time without transplanting. Before winter set in, a meagre harvest took place two months after the usual harvest period. At least they had food for some months, but that was a hard year.

There was a good reason why people daily visited their fields once the transplanted paddy began to bear grain and the ears of paddy became visible. Regulating the water in the fields was so important, and the plants needed to stand in ankle deep water in the first months. Although they dug channels and directed small streams of water to irrigate their fields, the water sources needed human help to ensure that the channels were not blocked by fallen leaves or soil. The farmers carried hoes and machetes and worked the waterways to their fields nearly every day. It was hard work but it made all the difference to the harvest. People in the village feared for their untended fields. If they lost the harvest, they would have to make perilous journeys to the plains to buy grain. It would entail travelling to the valley settlements with cotton, sugarcane and chillies to barter for rice and salt. The alternative to that was to borrow grain from neighbouring villages and repay them from the next year's harvest. To do that they would have to work doubly hard to get a bumper harvest that would pay off the loan. True, they had stocks of hill rice, but not in great quantities; the harvest from the terrace fields was sorely needed to supplement the hill rice. These thoughts about their rice fields weighed the people down.

Choba was convinced that theirs was not the only village affected by the darkness. His house had an attic where they stored their ornaments and head dresses. When he climbed up to it and peered through the small window, he could not make out any area unaffected by the scourge. It looked so hopeless. Would all this end in a famine?

Sunshine in these months was needed just as much as the rain. The best rice-growing months were the wet and hot months that were so uncomfortable for humans but so conducive to rice. When there was enough rain and heat, the paddy doubled in height and the stalks filled out with grain. Surely the dark and the drought would cause irreparable damage to the fields.

These worries made people feel very depressed. 'What does it matter if the spirits kill us off? If we survive, but have no grain, hunger can just as well bring a slower death.' People spoke foolishly like that. What was more terrible? The inexorable darkness or the desolation that was settling into people's spirits?

It was so much worse now than the spirit-grain-pounding time, though that was horrendous enough for those who went through it. Tola could still remember spending sleepless nights many years ago, holding onto her mother, because the spirits kept them awake with their grain pounding. She recounted this story to Thongdi and Namu:

'All night long, for many nights on end, the village was haunted by the sound of pestles pounding grain in wooden mortars. It was clearly the work of spirits for no mortal pounded grain at night for fear that such an unnatural activity would cause famines to visit them. Grain pounding after sunset is a big taboo for the household. Women were held responsible for upholding this taboo. My mother always made sure that our house had sufficient husked grain, and her daily routine included a couple of hours of grain-pounding. When the nightly pounding sounds came, no one could sleep. Children woke up and whimpered at the sound; parents dared not go out to investigate. I was only six or six and a half years then. I clung to my mother and refused to go anywhere alone. When morning came, the elders never found anything. My father performed ritual after ritual trying to uncover the meaning of the nocturnal visitations. He gave instructions that no one was to fetch water from the water source before him; very early the next morning, he rose before the light came and brought back unsullied water. He then cleansed the community house first and followed it up with cleansing of our house, the seer's house. A whole week of cleansing went by before he had a visitor; a tall, imposing man who had no face. My father told us that his flesh froze at the dreadful sight, but he was seer, and he pressed down his revulsion and pushed his spirit forward to hear the message his spirit visitor had brought.

'When it was over, he pulled on his black body-cloth and went to rouse the headman. It was not yet dawn, but this could not wait for day to break. They assembled all the people together, including the old and the infirm. When they were all gathered in the square, my father explained in his taciturn way that the grain-pounding was a warning. They were being warned to stay alert because a great enemy would come by night to attack them. Just as the spirit grain-pounding was keeping them awake at night, and leaving them listless in the day, this enemy would try to overpower them by exhausting them physically. When they were thoroughly worn down and unable to fight back, it would destroy them under cover of darkness.

'"What shall we fight our enemy with?" the headman had asked. "Are they men or are they spirits?"

'The seer had given him a strange look. "They are both," was his cryptic reply.

'The hearts of the men and women who heard his words were filled with dismay, and the headman pleaded, "Teach us how to defeat them." But my father turned and walked towards his house.

'Angrily the headman followed him home. "You have to teach us how to fight or we will be ruined and you along with the rest of us!"

"'I have no answers now," my father replied testily. "I need time to seek."

"'Well, don't take too long," was the headman's parting shot. We were frightened when we saw the two of them talking to each other in this manner. They were both very angry and we had never seen them thus before.

'In the coming days, just as the visitor had forewarned, the men lay awake at night full of foreboding at what lay ahead of them. In the day they were sluggish because they had not slept well, and sometimes fights broke out amongst the younger members. My father saw all this and called them together: "This will not do," he admonished them. "I am not hiding anything from you. Surely you know that my knowledge is not my own. I am a mediator, a channel between man and spirit. And that is how you should use me. Be here this evening and every evening from now on."

'The village was attacked by three female spirits. They were warrior spirits whose owners were not far behind them, mercenaries who were waiting to sack the village after the three had forced their way inside its walls. But the villagers had been preparing themselves for this encounter. They had kept themselves from conjugal pleasures, tasted no brew for many days, performed all the right rituals and strengthened their hearts. When the attackers finally appeared, the spirits were hideous to look at and the unready would have been quite paralysed at the sight of them. The only thing to indicate that they were female spirits were their waist cloths and blackened breasts. All three had long matted hair and their eyes burned red as they sought out their prey. If anything, they looked even more ghastly than their male counterparts. Each female spirit carried a short spear with its tip sharpened so keenly that it glinted in the dark. But the villagers were ready. Lifting their shields, they began to march toward the approaching spirits and when they were so close that they could easily have been speared they began to chant collectively. With one heart they cursed the spirits; they were fearless as they bent the spirits to their will, and the owners of the spirits watched the incredible sight of the three sinking powerlessly to the ground. Emboldened by this sight, the people chanted louder and louder, and their voices were as one, unified in killing the common threat to their homes and families. The owners, watching from a distance, saw that their champions were completely defeated, and their hearts shrank within them and they ran off without waiting to see more. The villagers saw who their real enemies were and the warriors chased them into the night where all of them met the fate they deserved.'

The fire was dying by the time Tola's story came to an end. Thongdi pushed a big piece of wood into the embers and thick smoke rose up over the fireplace.

In the village, the children had grown up hearing this story as it was told to them repeatedly. It was called the spirit-grain-pounding time. And every male-child was told this story to make his heart big inside him. The children listened attentively to this story each time it was told, and when the teller came to the part where the men bent the spirits to their will, the children would cheer so loudly the teller could not finish his story.

But this dark time was very different from anything they had ever known. They didn't know what to do. Only their seer could help them. And maybe his grandmother. But times had changed, and the new generation was thick-eared. Would they listen? If they listened, would they obey?

After the twentieth day passed, the seer's instructions for the people to cleanse themselves of ill thoughts came as a harsh rebuke. It was not received well. It fell on stony ground and bounced off and mocked the speaker where it lay.

'What shall I do, Grandmother?' Namu asked, his face downcast. 'They are no longer interested in saving themselves.'

Tola was quiet for a while. She was expecting this. She had been warned of the part she must play, but she had been putting it off, hoping it might not come to this.

'Let me try, Namu.'

Namu was torn between relief and despair. If they did not listen to their seer, what were the chances that they would listen to an old woman with no official standing? But he knew that in the village, his grandmother was respected for her wisdom. 'Yes, please try.'

'Help me to the door,' she said, reaching out her hand to him.

'No! You mustn't go out, Grandmother. No one must go out!'

'I won't go out, but I need my voice to carry and it will carry best when I am seated by the door.' She was referring to the slats in the door that let in air. Thongdi carried her chair to the door and placed it directly in front of the door. Next, Namu and Thongdi supported Tola on either side and helped her to her chair. When Thongdi pushed the two slats open, there was no wind outside. It was good – her voice would carry best if there was nothing to obstruct it. She sat there for some minutes clearing her throat. Then she began to sing a dirge. Namu and Thongdi were mystified by her singing. Dirges were only sung at deaths. Wasn't it a taboo to sing a dirge when there was no death in the family? Wouldn't that invite death? They threw worried looks at each other, and Thongdi signalled frantically that Namu should stop his grandmother.

The dark time had also become a time of deep silence. People spoke in muted voices at home. The usual village sounds had long since been smothered by the tomb-like gloom. There was none of the babble of children playing, the cacophony of dogs barking, or the squawking of the chickens – it had become as still as a ghost village. The only sound heard in their waking hours was the dirge when it was sung to announce a death. Tola's dirge singing carried across the village. It was the sound best carried by silence, because death always stopped anyone in their tracks. Who is it this time? They would wonder and they would stop all movement and sit quietly and strain to hear the words of the dirge.

That was what happened when Tola began singing. People tensed and listened when they heard the familiar notes of the dirge rising above the roofs. At first the words were indistinct. Then they heard Tola's name being repeated and they looked at each other and said, 'Oh no, old lady Tola has died!' But as they kept listening, they couldn't recognise the singing voice as that of Thongdi. It was Tola herself! In amazement, they listened as she sang on. She sang them her story. She sang them the history of their village, the story of the massacre and how the survivors rebuilt the village, and she sang them her visions. Her voice held them entranced.

'Children of *Shumang Laangnyu Sang,* listen to my story for I am the village. You call me *Kuneibü nyu,* our mother. I am indeed your mother. I have carried your stories from the very beginning and will carry them long after you are gone. I am all the women whose husbands have died young. I am all the women who have buried their dead babies in the cold ground. And I am all the men and women and children that have wanted this village to live. I am every word that chooses life and refuses death. Listen to your mother Tola, listen to your mother, the village.'

She sang the dirge for hours, and no one tried to stop her. She ended the funeral song by making the plea to her listeners to cleanse themselves of fearful and suspicious thoughts. She bade them protect their spirits so that the village could live again.

'A mother can live only through her children. And life can come only when room is made for life by pushing out thoughts of death and self-destruction. You have allowed your fears to press you down, but the time has now come to cast that weapon into the fire. I cannot do it for you, but you can do it for yourself. Let us stop hating, stop fearing, most of all, let us stop all complaining and all ill speaking. A village cannot be killed if its people continually choose to speak words of life into it. Death may try to come from outside; but real death begins internally, in the heart of man. Choose life, my children, choose wisely, choose the power that is there in life.'

When she ended, her head hung down in exhaustion. Quickly Namu and Thongdi helped her to her bed. Thongdi insisted that she remain in bed while she made some soup. Stoking the fire into flames, Thongdi boiled a cupful of water in a pot, added salt and crushed country ginger, and tasted it off the ladle. She added some more salt and quickly broke an egg into the water, stirring it until the egg solidified. Tola drank all of the soup and slept through the night.

People were greatly moved by Tola's dirge. They felt inspired by the accounts of what their ancestors had done after the massacre. The stories of human kindness shamed them into being less selfish, and more caring of others. The more prudent among them recognised that they were not doing much good to themselves by blaming each other for their present situation. Tola's words were repeated to each other in the different households by its members. Mothers taught them to their children and fathers tried to practise what she had said. Not everyone accepted what they had heard. But for the time being, there were hearts in each of the houses who wanted to practise what Tola had preached. *Let us stop hating, stop envying and blaming, most of all, let us stop complaining and all ill speaking.* Let us be the ones to love first, they would say to themselves. If it was going to help in bringing back the light, they would try their best to control themselves.

Chapter Fourteen

The darkness continued. But after Tola's dirge singing, it was as though a cloud had been lifted from people's minds. They were still trapped inside their homes but they were making the effort to think brightly. For the first time, a sense of excitement had been generated at what they would find after the darkness. In the past weeks, they had not dared think beyond that, so desperate were they. But now there was a shift in the atmosphere, and it was difficult not to feel the hope that Tola's song had resurrected in them.

Surely the end of the darkness would be like waking up to the world on the day of the creator-deity when he was seen crossing from mountain to mountain carrying the fierce animals on his shoulders. They remembered being told how their ancestor, newly born, had laughed and laughed at the sight of the two elephants squirming and bellowing as the creator held them in the crook of his arm and made his way into the deep woods. Would things look the same or would they find another earth in its place? Would they still find trees for there had been no trees until he stubbed out holes in the first earth and spat into them, and the Needlewood trees sprang up first, but they were so swiftly overtaken by the native oaks, so much so that the elephant grass had to stop their profligate growth and allot them their rightful places. Surely everything would look very different. It would certainly feel much altered. Would they get the old sun back? Or would it be a new sun? Like the first sun and the first moon that the creator had moulded in the palm of his hand and flung into the dark, formless skies?

Surely on the day the sun returned, they would all sing together the song of the creator-deity that they were taught from childhood, for everyone knew how to sing it:

Mountain maker
Mountain maker
It was your hand
Your mighty hand
That set down the mountains
Over the plainlands

Your mighty hand
That placed the rocks and trees
On the mountain slopes
And the short wild grass
Over the treeless heights
Mountain maker
Mountain maker
Fathering the skies
Mothering the rivers
And the fields in the valleys
Mountain maker mountain maker
We give you all glory
Shambulee Shambulee Shambulee.

It was a song sung by grown-ups, but the children loved to join in at the refrain, their little voices calling out *Shambulee, Shambulee,* long after the song was over.

They could all see for themselves that it had already begun. Every now and then people checked what they had said. If a complaint was voiced, the speaker was heard apologising a few moments later. *The inner darkness is being dispelled*, Tola was heard saying with a small smile. Though she never left the house, her spirit could sense the repentance that was sweeping across the village, house by house, soul by soul.

Early on in the darktime, the headman had started to beat a gong every morning to announce a new day. It was used as the signal to light the fire and prepare meals. As they entered the third week, people became more cautious with their food stores. Meals were cut down to one a day that they ate in the afternoon hours. If they felt hungry after that, they snacked on boiled lentils and maize. Most families had killed and eaten their chickens as the dark time began. They now debated on whether it was time to take out the *food of war*, millet. Some families alternated millet with rice. This was a sort of war, after all, they argued. Even if they were not being attacked by enemy warriors with spears and *daos*, the constant onslaught of darkness and spiritual warfare was fraught with tension not very different from physical battles.

Their movements had become very restricted. It was a drastic change from the active lives they had always led. No more getting up early to get ready for the field. No back-breaking digging and planting and weeding. No carrying back firewood and pumpkins and tapioca, or any of the other vegetables they had planted in their jhum fields. The leisurely life was so different from what they had visualised it to be. They fretted to be outdoors again. Their bodies groaned at the forced sedentary life under their roofs. Their beloved homes had become their prisons. But there was nothing to be done. They had to learn the lesson of waiting. And they learned it best as they applied themselves to waiting actively. It was as the seer of Mvüphri had said, *waiting must be accompanied by an attitude of seeking and receiving wisdom.* Although they were not fully aware of it, that was what the people were beginning to do.

At the same time, life had grown more dangerous than ever. Wild animals came right up to the village gate trying to push it open. They had heard the grunts of wild elephants. One day, a bear had spent many hours scratching the walls. Men got their spears ready inside their houses. If it broke through, they would use their spears to defend their families. But, in truth, the walls were sturdier than they looked. Their fathers had seen to that in their time. The only area where it was weak was at the west end of the village; but there had been no time to mend that. One could only hope that no intruder would find that weak spot. At least they felt they would be safe from wild animals so long as they stayed inside the village. The biggest problem was the spirits. Every village gate was protected against spirit entry by spells cast by the seer. The more powerful the seer, the stronger the gate. Namu's village gate was almost powerless against spirits.

When Namu heard that spirits were roaming the spaces between the houses and killing people, he was not shocked. In his new position, he knew so much more. He hoped that it would all end soon. It wasn't easy to keep holding out against the continuous battering that their faiths received. After Tola's dirge chanting day, they had heard no more of the melancholic death melody. It meant that there had been no more deaths. It was nothing short of a miracle.

However, a few days later, towards morning, they heard a vile sound. It echoed round the whole village. It was a blood-curdling cry, beastly and utterly unnerving. The men looked for their weapons, but no one actually dared to go out and investigate. As they were hesitating, some other sounds were heard – the smashing of bamboo walls and the agonised cries of a man being subjected to gruesome torture came from the western part of the wall. Namu and Choba rushed out of their houses. They carried their spears in one hand and their wormwood torches in the other. At first, they could not see anything. The two drew closer to the place where the sounds had come from. The sight that met their eyes froze their hearts. A giant tiger had a man in his grip, and the hapless man began screaming again. The two men charged the tiger, shouting and throwing their spears at him. Namu's spear missed, but Choba's spear went through his ribcage. The tiger roared in pain and let the man go. For some terrifying seconds, the tiger turned his attention on the two as though it would charge them, but it suddenly swerved around and sped off into the darkness.

The man was beyond help. He had been no match for the beast. It had broken off the wall behind the man's house and smashed his bamboo house as though it were made of cardboard. Neither Namu nor Choba had ever seen such a great tiger. It was gigantic and yet it hardly made a sound as it bounded off into the forest with a spear-point between its ribs. By the light of wormwood torches, they quickly buried the victim. Choba's instructions that no one was to come outside were heeded. They could not perform the death rituals; the dead were to be disposed of immediately for the safety of the living. The bereaved would have to mourn in private. This was an unnatural season and everyone was aware of that. Maybe one day when the dark ended, they could mourn their dead officially.

Choba followed Namu home. 'Aunt!' he called when he saw Tola sitting by the fire and waiting for them.

'Choba! How good to see you even though it is such a grim time.'

'Aunt! Tell us how to act. Advise us, teach us what next to do. Strengthen our hearts with your words!'

'Ah Choba, I should be the one to ask you what we shall do.' Tola sighed.

'No Aunt. We are like children wandering in the woods and behind every tree is a spirit waiting to kill us. Today, the tiger that killed the man was such a huge beast. I have never seen anything like it. It was enormous. It took off with my spear still inside it.'

'The darkness aids dark things to grow. The only way to defeat it is to hold on to the wisdom of choosing what to fear and what to stop fearing.'

Choba looked confused. 'I thought you said we should reject all our fears, Aunt.'

'Yes, I did, and I meant it. We should reject all our fears, all but one, fear of the creator deity. That is the fear that will stop us from profaning the sacred.'

'Aunt, what do you mean? Are you saying we should not fear the tiger?' Choba lowered his voice. 'Tonight, when I saw the tiger, I thought I would die!'

'You should not fear any creature of the dark. Come here my son.' She beckoned to him to come sit beside her. 'We are obstructed by our fears from becoming all that we are. We are shackled by our fears, you see.'

'I'll try and remember that, Aunt.'

'You have some other spears I hope?' Tola asked.

'I do.'

'Better get them ready,' she said with a knowing look. 'The tiger is your fear. He is the fears of the whole village. You have to transcend yourselves in order to kill him.'

Chapter Fifteen

They repaired the breach in the wall as best they could. They knew the tiger would come back, but they did not know when. Seeing that it was no ordinary tiger, they wondered if it would be frightened away by a great fire. As a rule, animals kept away from fires. Namu sharpened his best spear and kept it ready, but Tola asked them to look among her things, and they found her father's spear. She gave the partially rusted spear to Namu. The wooden handle was splintered at the base.

'It belonged to your great-grandfather. It is the spear of a seer,' she said. Namu took it reverently and cleaned it so thoroughly that the spearhead glinted after he had sharpened the metal. The wooden handle was easily replaced with a new one. Namu whittled it from a shaft of hard native oak wood he had kept aside for just such a purpose.

'I have a brand-new spear now!' he exclaimed, lifting it so the others could see it by the light from the fireplace.

'May the creator help you kill the tiger with it,' Tola proclaimed.

'May the creator help me to kill the tiger,' Namu agreed.

The next night, the villagers heard a wrenching sound. The chilling cry seemed to come from the headman's house. Was Choba being attacked? Namu ran out with his spear and torch.

But he could not see anything at first. Choba came out of his house, his spear upraised.

'I thought the sound came from your house!' Namu said.

'And I thought it came from yours!' Choba exclaimed.

The men instinctively looked around them but they saw nothing. Where did the awful sound come from? Surely it was the tiger.

As if in reply to their question, it came again, this time from behind the village gate. They saw two bright lights glowing in the dark, and they waited for the tiger to spring or try to break through the wall as it had done the other night.

But the great beast turned away from the village and began to walk in the direction of the woods. At first, Choba and Namu were utterly confused. The tiger carried on for a few meters more before it stopped and turned back, its fierce eyes burning through the dark, watching them. The tiger continued to do this, sauntering off a little distance, then stopping to look back and wait as though it was signalling them to follow.

All off a sudden Namu cried out, 'We can't wait any longer!' He began to run to the gate so Choba had no choice but to follow him. He was fumbling to open the gate, but it was designed in such a way that it could not be opened or closed by one man alone.

'Namu! I forbid you to go out!' Choba shouted. At Choba's shouting, his son Mongba came running.

'If you don't help me, it will come back and kill us all! Help me open the gate. I have to do this!'

Choba saw that it was useless trying to stop Namu. Together they lifted the heavy gate open and Namu passed into the darkness and was quickly lost from view. Hesitantly, Choba and

Mongba pushed the gate back into place. But Mongba's heart was torn.

'Father, shouldn't I follow him?' he asked. Namu was taking an immense risk, and Mongba felt it his duty to share his friend's fate. But Choba sternly forbade him.

'He is seer. You are not. He will know what to do.'

Namu ran like a madman down the path, ululating loud war cries that echoed back to the village. He kept running until the tiger loomed in front of him, the fire from its eyes searing Namu's skin, causing him to throw away the wormwood torch. Namu held up his great-grandfather's spear and kept charging on. At the last moment, the tiger opened its mouth so wide that Namu ran headlong into it. He had no time to recognise the fact that there was no darkness inside the mouth of the tiger. Confused, yet ever ready to kill the tiger Namu kept running down what looked like the path from the village to the field. Up ahead he saw a figure at a bend in the road. Namu clutched his spear tightly, ready to defend himself if the man should attack him. But the stranger turned to face him and for one bewildering moment Namu thought he was looking into a mirror. The man was the spitting image of himself! He stopped in his tracks trying to make sense of it, but the other person didn't seem surprised at all.

'Namu!' a woman's voice called out joyously. He looked for the owner of the voice, and a woman walked out into his path, nimbly stepping in front of the man. She held out her hands, and came up to Namu, pulled him close to her and brought his head to rest on her shoulder. Namu was entirely confused. He did not know what to do. What had happened to the tiger? And who were these two? How did they know him? Why did he feel that they were not strangers?

'Finally, you have come,' the woman whispered as she gazed at him. She was very beautiful and the two of them, both the man and the woman, called him by name. They seemed to know him very well.

'Namu, our beloved,' the woman continued, looking deep into his eyes.

Namu's mind was racing. Who could this woman be? She knew who he was, and he felt there was something oddly familiar about the two of them.

'My son, my son, how I have waited for this moment.'

Did he hear that right? Why was she calling him her son? Could this beautiful woman be his mother?

'Yes, I am Sechang, your mother,' she said as if she could read his thoughts.

Sechang! Then the man had to be none other than his father, Topong Nyakba who had been killed in the massacre.

'Are you really – are you my parents?' He got the words out with some difficulty. He looked from one to the other, and they both smiled lovingly back at him.

'Yes, we are your father and mother, dearest Namu, and we have been waiting for you all these years. Come here my son. Come, I will tell you all.' She took Namu by the hand and drew Namu's head close to her and he let her.

'Look, this is indeed your father,' she said as she pointed towards Topong Nyakba. The pride in her voice was unmistakable. 'He was the handsomest young man of his age-group. Look at him, isn't he still so handsome? When he came courting me, I could not refuse him, even if he were from another village, I could not find the word 'no' in those days. We waited until the harvest was over and at the harvest festival we were married. Do you know our village? Our old village? *Shumang Laangnyu*. It was the happiest place on earth. That was where we lived. Your father and I and your grandmother. No one was happier than us.' She smiled at Namu and her face radiated all the joy that a mother is capable of showing over a child who was lost but is found again.

Sechang then turned and walked away from Namu further down the path. 'Come and meet your sisters!' she called.

'I have sisters?' No one had told him he had siblings. It was irresistible.

'Yes, of course!' Sechang replied enthusiastically. 'Come!'

The two of them ran down the road holding hands, Topong Nyakba following them closely.

His mother's village was nothing like his village. The houses were not built close together but set wide apart and flowers bloomed in front of many of the houses. The great-roofed houses of wealthy men were much bigger and many of the houses displayed heads of cattle, the decorations used by title-takers. He saw men sitting in the outer yards of the houses, holding brew horns.

In front of them was the house of a title-taker. Outside on the wide porch, there were three men seated and drinking from their brew-horns. 'There's your grandfather.' His mother pointed casually at a grey-haired man who was taller than the rest. The man came forward when he saw them.

'It is Namu, isn't it? Welcome, welcome my grandson! You must stay as long as you want!' Namu stared up at the man who had called him 'grandson.' He was smiling back at him with kind eyes. Namu's hand in his large hand was like that of a child, and his grandfather reached down and patted his head before re-joining his guests.

'We're nearly home,' his mother said as she drew him toward a house to the side of the wide-roofed house of his grandfather.

Two little girls were playing in the front yard and when they saw him coming, they ran to him squealing with delight and calling out, 'Namu! Namu!' They threw themselves at him and all of them tumbled to the ground laughing and holding on to one another. When they had calmed down, Namu stood up and found that he could reach only to his mother's waist. Greatly surprised he looked at a reflection of himself in the window and realised he had had become a ten-year-old boy. He was the child Namu again, but this time with a difference. It appeared as though he was being given the chance to relive his childhood with the family he had never known.

His two sisters were twins, Noni and Loni. Namu had trouble telling them apart, but Loni showed him a little mole on her right cheek which Noni did not have.

'Mother said you are a hunter. Will you show us how to hunt?' It was Noni.

'But you are girls. I don't know if girls are allowed to hunt,' Namu replied.

'Don't worry. We will ask Mother and she will say yes.'

Namu was amused at the determined look on Noni's face. Of the two, Noni was clearly the acknowledged leader. Loni said yes to everything her sister suggested and that was what kept the peace between them. The girls loved him. Every now and then they would stop their play and come to him and stroke his hair and lean on his shoulder. The way they called his name was so tender, so loving, no one had ever called him like that before. It was true that Tola had brought him up with great love, but this was altogether different. After all his mother was his mother and she coddled him the way mothers are allowed to coddle sons, and his sisters would not let him out of their sight. If one had to go and fetch something, the other held on to his arm and sang to him. Namu thought his sisters were the sweetest girls he had ever seen. Noni was running back to them as fast as her little legs could carry her.

'Mother says yes,' she panted. 'Can we start now?'

'Start what?' Namu was puzzled.

'You said you would teach us to hunt!'

'Oh that.' Namu had forgotten all about it. 'Let's go and find some wood to whittle into spears and bows and arrows.'

The girls helped him collect wood and they let out little whoops of delight at the tiny spears and arrows that their brother was shaping. They took their bows and arrows and romped all over the village shooting at anything they found interesting, stones, grass, and big leaves.

'Namu look! I shot a deer!'

'Namu look! I have killed a bear!' They would shout every time they hit a leaf or a stone. They made a game of it, saying that stones were big animals and leaves were smaller animals, and berries were birds.

'But we can't use birds for food!' Loni said quite unhappily. She looked as though she were about to cry. Namu stroked her cheek and soothed her, promising they would not shoot the birds and if they did so accidentally, he would tend them back to health. It brought a smile back to her little face and Namu felt such affection in his heart for his two sisters. He wanted to protect them from any hurt or harm. How he loved them!

There was little time to sit and ponder over all the questions this trip had raised in him. The girls were so active that they kept him on his toes and they roamed all over the village as they showed him every corner of their mother's village. Namu wondered why the houses were so much bigger than other village houses. A man walked past them herding cattle. The animals were giant beasts. Yet they allowed the man to lead them into the shed where he tied them up for the night.

There was a house where a woman was sitting with her baby and dandling it. They heard the child's laughter from a long way off. When they came near, Namu saw that the mother was doing something that made the little baby chortle in glee. The mother kept this up for what seemed like hours and they could see that the baby was exhausted by it, but it couldn't stop chortling. The girls were mesmerised by the laughing baby, but it made Namu uneasy because he had seen the baby gasp for air whenever it finished laughing.

'Come let's go on, Noni, Loni, I want to see some more of the village,' he said pulling his sisters away.

A few houses later, an old woman called to them. 'Noni! Loni! Come here! I have something for you!'

'It's Grandmother Chemden. She always gives us treats. Come on!' They ran up eagerly to the house.

'Come and sit down here beside me.' The old woman patted the bench on which she was sitting. 'Who is your guest?'

'It's Namu, Grandmother, he is our brother.'

'Oh Namu! Of course, it is. I know him. How big you have grown Namu! We have all been waiting for you.'

Namu was very surprised. The village had simply embraced him and every member was greeting him in such a welcoming manner.

'I have something for you, Namu,' the old woman got up and reached for her walking stick.

'For me, Grandmother Chemden? Did you know I was coming here today?'

'Oh yes, we all knew,' she said as she disappeared into her bedroom. The old woman came back with a rounded object that was brown in colour and had ridges down the side.

'What is it Grandmother Chemden?' he asked curiously.

'It is a memory ball. It stores your memories and you can use it to recall every memory you have ever made with your loved ones.'

'Oh it sounds marvellous. And you want to give it to me?' he had to ask again.

'Oh yes. I have been waiting for you to show up.'

'Thank you, Grandmother Chemden. I will take good care of it.' Namu held it in the palm of his hand and peered at it. It was soft and malleable and when he turned it over, it made a rolling movement.

'Ai! Is it some kind of animal?' he asked with rounded eyes.

'No. But it is a living entity, you know. It is a memory ball of life.'

Namu thanked her and put the ball in his pocket.

The old woman now seemed impatient for the children to be off. 'Come back tomorrow, and Namu, don't lose that.'

They thanked her and ran off. Now they were at the *morung*, the big community hall. The massive wooden door was open, and Namu took a peek at the hall, but it was quite dark inside. There were steps leading up to the *morung,* but they looked very steep. A child could not possibly climb them.

'Have you ever been inside?' Namu asked his sisters.

'Of course not,' Noni replied. 'It's not a place for children. Not even for women. Only our father goes to the *morung*. You're a boy. You can go when you are older.'

Namu craned his neck to get another look at the interior of the *morung*, and when he did that, he saw several human heads hanging in a row. Some were still dripping blood and the ones hanging just inside the door fixed their eyes on him. He gasped in fright, and he caught his sisters by the hand and began to drag them with him. But when they were some distance from the *morung,* his curiosity overcame him and he looked over his shoulder at the community hall. There was nothing there. The grisly sight he had seen a few moments ago had vanished.

'Children! Children!' It was Sechang coming to fetch them. Noni and Loni ran to their mother while Namu hung back, but not for long. He imitated his sisters and ran to hug their mother.

'It's late now. We must go home and eat. Namu must be so hungry.'

Namu's family lived in a smaller house next to their grandfather's. There was no huge jutting roof over their house. Their father was not a title-taker. When they were seated at the kitchen around the fire, he smiled at his son and said,

'Eat well son. Your mother and I are very happy you have come home.'

'We too, we too!' his sisters piped up. His mother had cooked a warm meal with mushrooms and country garlic. It was very filling and Namu felt terribly sleepy after eating.

'You are tired, dearest son,' his mother said in a soothing voice. 'Come and lie down here and rest.' She made a bed for him beside her own bed and picked him up in her arms. Namu felt like he was sinking into a deep darkness, but it was very restful, for it was his mother's womb.

Sechang continued to carry her son and she began to sing in a soft voice; it was a lullaby that he remembered from his childhood and it soothed him so that he fell asleep right there on her lap inside the opened mouth of the tiger.

Chapter Sixteen

Namu was gone for a full two days. Thongdi was inconsolable, and Tola was extremely worried. She knew he was in very great danger. Whenever she tried to reach him, a wall would come up and there was no response.

'Is he still alive?' Thongdi asked with great anxiety.

Choba had not left their house since the day Namu ran out and leaped at the tiger. He repeated Thongdi's question.

'Is he?'

'He is alive, but he needs our help to get him out soon,' Tola replied.

'But how can we help? We don't even know where they are!' Choba looked dismayed. He had exhausted every resource he had.

'Aunt, you are our only hope,' Choba begged. Tola knew this was coming. Deep inside, Tola knew she was the only one who could save him. That is, if he still wanted to be saved.

She had known since the moment that Namu leaped into the tiger's mouth that she would have to leap with him.

'Listen carefully then,' she said to Choba and Thongdi. 'I am going to go after him, and you must not be alarmed at anything I say or do. Promise me you won't try to wake me if you see me looking as if I were dead. It's so important that no one disturbs me. This is the only way to save him.'

The other two assured her they would do as she said. They positioned themselves beside her bed as if guarding her. She had lain down, but sat up again as if remembering something.

'Do not disturb me on any account. Do not allow anyone to enter the house. They will try to deceive you.' She fixed her eyes on the other two waiting for their response.

'We will do as you say, Aunt.'

Then Tola did something that she had watched her father do a long time ago. It was extremely dangerous for the person but it was the only thing to do. Spreading a mat on the earthen floor, Tola lay down as one dead, relinquishing her flesh completely, and while in that state, she sent her spirit to find Namu. Thongdi was horrified to see that Tola had stopped breathing, but she forced herself to remember the instructions they had received, and restrained herself.

As if from a great distance Namu heard his grandmother calling him. He didn't want to answer her. It was so wonderful lying in his mother's lap and listening to her song-stories, he didn't want it to ever stop.

'Namu! Namu!' Tola's voice grew louder until she was at the entrance of the tiger's mouth.

'Namu! Kill the tiger! He is your greatest enemy! Kill him now!' Tola shouted.

Namu tried to shut out his grandmother's voice. He put his hands over his ears and turned his head away. Was Tola quite mad? Why would she drag him away from his family now that he had found them? Nothing would tear him away from his adorable sisters and his loving mother and father. They were so happy he was here. Didn't Tola want him to be happy?

'Namu! Namu!' Tola shouted even louder. Namu got up abruptly. He would tell her to leave. He would tell her he wasn't ever going to come back. As a matter of fact, he would invite her to join them! As Namu got up, he saw his spear at the edge of the bed. He reached for it automatically and stood up. His mother followed him, watching his every move.

'Namu, if you kill the tiger, we will die,' his mother was pleading.

Her words shocked Namu and left him confused. Why wouldn't his mother want him to kill the tiger? How did she even know about the tiger? The hair on his neck prickled.

'Don't, Namu, don't kill the tiger. You will never see us again if you kill him,' she continued with tears in her eyes.

'Don't cry Mother, I never want to hurt you.' Namu meant that.

Topong Nyakba came close to his son.

'My son, we have longed so much for this reunion,' he joined Semang in pleading. Topong Nyakba placed his hands on Namu's shoulders and Namu felt his fingers digging into him. Topong Nyakba's face turned hard and unsmiling.

'I am your father. I forbid you to kill the tiger. Obey me, Namu.'

Namu looked at his father. Topong Nyakba began to age before his eyes. He was no longer the handsome young warrior that he had first appeared to be. He now looked gaunt and cadaverous, his eyes burning into Namu.

'Don't do it son, you are one of us, don't you see?'

At his father's words something snapped in Namu's head.

No! He was not one of them! Whatever they were.

He looked at his father again. But his countenance was so changed he was unrecognisable. Topong Nyakba was advancing towards his son with murderous rage in his eyes. 'We have shared a meal together! You are one of us. You will not leave, do you hear me Namu?'

'Namu!' It was Tola again. She called him in the voice he knew from his childhood, the authoritative voice that always pulled him back to safety. And now it was calling him to sanity.

Whatever emotions and sentiments had been stirred up in him by the meeting with his family were forgotten in that instant. Namu leaped away from his father's lunge, and he raced out the way he had come in, his feet barely touching the ground.

As he reached the entrance, he thrust his spear with all his might into the tiger's mouth, and leaped out just in time before the giant mouth clamped shut.

Both he and Tola saw his father and mother weeping as the tiger died. Namu's beautiful little sisters were wild-eyed with grief. Namu trembled all over. It was the first time in his life that he had known fear. It slowed him down, and his knees shook uncontrollably. But Tola came and shouted in his ear, 'Run! Run as fast as you can!' With pounding heart, he ran clear of the area where the tiger lay dead. But the darkness was all around him, and it slowed him down. 'Grandmother, help me!' he cried out. 'Namu follow my voice!' she shouted and he ran into the places where he could hear her calling until at last, he came to the partly opened gate and jumped inside.

Tola had been lying on the floor for hours as still as a corpse. When Namu reached the safety of the village, Thongdi and Choba heard her cough and she began to receive her spirit back into her body. Her tremendous effort had worked and in turn, it had saved the village. Nevertheless, it was an exercise for which she would pay dearly. It would be many weeks before her body recovered from the ordeal of being abandoned. Yet what cared she for that when her beloved grandson had been rescued, and the power of the tiger destroyed.

When she returned to her flesh, Thongdi rubbed her limbs with oil, trying to restore warmth and hasten the process of resurrection. Tola's body was stone cold, and as the blood flowed back, she grimaced at the manner in which the spirit fought at being overpowered by the flesh. Thongdi kept on rubbing. Very gradually, the iciness receded, but the younger woman did not stop her ministrations. She had still not recovered from seeing Tola lying motionless, not drawing breath for many hours, and her resuscitation was no less than a return from the dead. When Tola tried to speak, she stuttered and could not get words out. It was only natural after the great cold her body had been subjected to, the cold of body-death. They fed her warm fluids and softly boiled rice to strengthen her, and the colour very gradually returned to her face.

When she was able to get up, Tola directed her energies to Namu who was still overwhelmed by the meeting with his family. 'They were not real,' she kept telling Namu. 'They were there to deceive you. Don't let anyone tell you that you have done anything wrong.'

Namu was sitting by the doorway, weeping over the traumatic parting from his family. He clung to every word that Tola was saying.

'Oh Grandmother, when Father said I was one of them I just knew I could not agree with him. They were all wrong and even if they were my father and my mother, I knew I had to get away from them. Yet why do I feel guilty? Did I do wrong?'

'You did right, Namu. They were not who they pretended to be. Go and rest your mind.'

'Ah but I felt so much love for them. Loni, Noni – my sweet, sweet little sisters, you would have loved them so much too,

Grandmother. And Mother and Father, no one ever told me how beautiful my mother was.'

A paroxysm of weeping came over Namu. He felt as though he had lost everything, everything. And it was all by his own hand. They let him be while he wept over his loss. Thongdi tried to stroke his back but he pushed her hand away and broke into wrenching sobs.

When he would not stop, Tola became very angry.

'Are you going to be defeated by a lie? By lies? How would Sechang and Topong Nyakba have been able to have more children when their bodily life was over? They were not real. None of them were real. This darkness is a spiritual darkness. Under cover of the darkness the spirits have been trying to kill us off. They have been doing it with intimidation and they have been doing it with every treacherous avenue they know.'

'Can that be true, Grandmother?' Namu looked up at Tola.

'Of course, it is. They knew you could not be intimidated with fearful sights as other men are, so they sought to attack you in that area where you are so vulnerable without your being aware of it. They provided you a semblance of the ideal family and the love that you always felt was missing from your life when you learned how your parents died.

'It cannot be something you have consciously sought, because you were too young to know. But it was sitting there deep inside you and they provided the perfect images at just the right time to deceive you. Precisely the very exact images, because spirits excel at deceiving.'

Namu looked perplexed. 'But I have never wanted any other family apart from you, Grandmother. I have not harboured dreams of a reunion with my parents.'

'As I said, you may not have done so consciously. But the mind is a strange country. It contains seeds for unborn thoughts.'

'So, all that was a lie?' Namu asked again. 'I felt so much love for my sisters, so much, and how they loved me. They wept as though they were dying when I left. You saw them too, Grandmother, you saw them. Are you sure that was all a lie?'

'How else would you find people inside a tiger's mouth let alone a whole village?'

Chapter Seventeen

'Namumolo has killed a tiger! Namumolo has killed a giant tiger!' Choba was shouting and people looked through the cracks in their houses and strained to see what was happening. It was excellent news, yet people were hesitant to leave their houses to hear more. Mongba and Bumo were the first to come out with their spears upraised. Slowly, the other young men joined them. The great danger was past. The gate was opened so the men could file out. All of them carried torches as they marched out. They found the body of the tiger in a clearing. The animal was colossal. It was sprawled out on the ground, looking massive even in death. The giant head lay with its mouth pierced through by Namu's spear.

Mongba drove his spear into the tiger's heart and jumped back in fright.

'It's still breathing!' he screamed. The other men came running with their spears and *daos. The tiger was still alive!* Choba lifted his wormwood torch high above the tiger. When he did that, he saw something move. It was the tail of the tiger.

'Cut off the tail!' he shouted. Choba had remembered that the power of a spirit tiger was in the tail and that it contained so much poison that if it flicked it at any creature, it would kill it. Mongba leapt to his father's side and chopped off the tiger's tail. He grabbed it and lifted it up for the others to see. But his victory was short-lived as another man shouted: 'There's another tail!'

Bumo grabbed the other tail and cut it off. In all, they cut off six tails from the body of the dead tiger. After the tails had been cut, they made very sure that the tiger would not be able to resurrect and plague them. The men brought all their wormwood torches and burnt the body of the tiger, piling wood atop it and letting the flames cover it very thoroughly. The fire lit up the whole forest, as though it were banishing the darkness. It burned until only ashes remained of the vile creature.

They put the tiger-tails into a basket and took them back to the village.

'Namu, fetch your grandmother!' Choba shouted.

Tola was already limping forward with Thongdi's help.

'Aunt, what is the meaning of this? The tiger has six tails!' Choba asked.

'Have you cut off all the tails? You must!'

'Yes, we have, Aunt.'

Tola looked at the tails and shuddered.

'Each tail stands for different forms of pride. Rebellion. Arrogance. Greed. Hatred of all that is good. Self-seeking. Envy. It's quite possible one tail represents more than one thing. You have now cut off all connection the tiger had to the spirit world.'

'Then it was right to kill the tiger!' Namu burst out in great relief. The last image he had of his weeping family members was so disturbing that Namu had still been inwardly plagued with guilt over killing the tiger.

'Oh yes it was. I believe we have done our part in helping the spirit world by killing the tiger,' Choba affirmed.

Choba had not finished speaking when a glow began to spread over the village. By this time, all the survivors had come out of their houses to hear the story of great victory. But when the light appeared, there was distress and alarm. The sounds of rejoicing stopped, and children whimpered at the new threat. People had been held captive for so long by the fear of the unknown that the growing light reignited their fears.

A scream broke through the silence. 'Watch out! It's another attack!'. But it was not an attack. It was the light returning to the land. It grew brighter and brighter until its glory was almost unbearable. They had been so long without light that when it came back it felt unnatural and forbidding. Mothers ran and plucked leaves with which they covered their children's eyes. Old men and women covered their heads with their cloths, but the light was so bright it penetrated the heavy weaves. They kept on watching, half expecting it to suddenly disappear as it had that day so long ago when everything turned into night. But this light continued to grow, and as it grew, its glow became diffused so it was not so harsh anymore.

'We are saved! The darkness is over!'

The excitement was infectious. It was day, it was normalcy, it was salvation. A little girl jumped up and down in joy. She started to clap her hands and sing loudly, and soon the older ones joined her. Their feet beat festive rhythms on the ground and the songs they sang covered the land like the blessings of raintime.

Meanwhile, the men took the six tails and burnt them at the same spot they had burned the tiger-body. They dug a deep pit and buried whatever remained of the tiger. They never wanted it to revive and besiege the village again. Over the pit, they collectively chanted curses against the forces of darkness that had brought the tiger to life.

'Women! Do you hear me, women! It is time to bring out your brew and worship the creator!' Choba shouted.

The women ran to their houses and returned bringing rice brew in earthen pitchers; they sprinkled it on the ground and all over the stone foundation of the village gate. Two women climbed up the blocks of stone that formed the base and splashed brew over the gate. It was their way of honouring the creator for delivering them. Later on, they would each sprinkle brew over their own houses and sanctify their dwelling places. When their worship was done, no one went indoors. They stood together watching the ball of white light in the skies. It seemed to grow bigger and whiter.

'What is it Aunt? That can't be the sun. It looks so white and weak,' Choba asked.

Tola leaned on her stick and stared at it. The whiteness was translucent. 'Ah, it is the shadow of the sun!' she said looking at the white circle grow. 'Keep watching! The sun will come running after its shadow!'.

The people shaded their eyes with their hands and continued to peer at the circle until suddenly a tiger appeared in the middle of the sky and regurgitated the sun from its belly. When it was finished, the tiger began to fall to earth, but their communal screaming prevented it from falling upon their village.

Chapter Eighteen

Half of the fields were ruined. The other half had survived where the water had not dried out, but the paddy was very badly undernourished. People worked very hard to get water to the dying paddy. They still hesitated to stay overnight at the field huts but they compensated by going to their fields many hours before first light and returned home in a big group before the stars came out. Some evenings, the groups would sing their way home.

Their efforts were rewarded when the wilting plants revived and they could save the grain on the stalks. But it would be a poor harvest that year, a very poor harvest. That was to be expected. They would be grateful if there was anything to harvest at all. In the end, they agreed, life was way more valuable than a good harvest.

About two days after the light returned, three men were seen walking down the field path and heading up the village path. It was Chongshen and the two men who had accompanied him to Mount Mvüphri. How happy everyone was to see them.

'Seer!' 'Seer!' people called out wherever he went for that was the way they used to address him before. 'The seer has come back!' the ones standing at the village square shouted for all to hear. Children clapped their hands and joined in the shouting. Women ran out of their houses to see this wonderful event. Even the old people came to the doors of their houses and peered at the men. Everyone had feared that the three men might have been killed by spirits. They were very touched by the welcome the villagers gave them.

Chongshen waved back at them. But once inside his house, he refused the ministrations of his family members and went directly to the headman's house.

'I cannot take any rest before I meet the headman,' he explained to his wife. She, in turn, had understood that his office would always be more important than his family and she did not try to stop him.

Choba greeted him warmly and bade him sit down. But Chongshen stood in the middle of the room and refused to sit saying he had something important to convey.

'What could be so important that you cannot do me the courtesy of sitting down in my house?' Choba pressed his visitor. Chongshen sat down reluctantly, stiff-backed and formal as if he were at a meeting of the village council.

'Choba, I'll not be seer anymore,' he announced.

Choba was taken aback. He was very relieved that Chongshen had survived the trip to Mvüphri, and he had presumed that things would go back to the old order now that Chongshen had returned. 'Why not?' Choba demanded.

'For the simple reason that I am not a seer. I thought I was, but my trip to Mvüphri has shown me that I am a charlatan. I am a farmer and I am a householder. I will be perfectly happy not to be seer any longer.'

It was a new Chongshen. Gone was the self-important middle-aged man who liked to be seen making chicken sacrifices and chanting long prayers over the offerings that the villagers brought to him every month. After making his confession, he managed to look almost carefree.

'What do you say?' he looked Choba in the eye.

'But who will be seer then? We need a seer. No village dare be without a seer.'

'Choba, listen, my uncle was seer before me. My cousin Tola was a dream-receiver long before I even made my first chicken sacrifice. In fact, it was Tola who came to me to tell me of the prophetic dreams she had received, but I advised her not to mention it to anyone. Do you know what happened after that? The darkness came! It found us totally unprepared because I had not heeded her dreams. You don't know about that, do you? You don't know how jealous I was of Tola's dreams and visions. I wanted to believe I was the real seer. Yes, her father was indeed my uncle, my mother's brother. Yet even if I was the closest surviving relative, I did not come from the line of seers. I flaunted my own dreams and made all of you think I had seer-blood in me. But I haven't, and the Seer of Mvüphri has made that all so apparent to me. He told me I was only the seer of the calendar and crops and festivals. And that it was Tola who was the seer over men's destinies! I don't want to continue this charade any more. It is not good for the village. Can't you see I had no wisdom to save the village from the darkness?'

'You still haven't answered my question,' Choba responded. He deliberately ignored Chongshen's revelation, although he had understood each and every word. 'Who will be seer then? Not Tola. Not because she is a woman, but she is old. She is ninety-four. Who knows how much longer she will be around?'

'Namu? Why not Namu? He is the great-grandson of a seer.'

This matter would take a bit longer to solve, Choba thought. Namu was young. He had the heart of a warrior-hunter. He would need much persuasion to relent to leading the secluded life of a seer. But he would speak to Namu about it, and he would enlist Tola's help in doing that.

'Go your way, Chongshen,' Choba pronounced in a kindly manner, 'and remember you can still serve the village through other avenues.' Choba was too generous a man to hold Chongshen's faults against him. Or maybe he felt guilty for having believed him, and ignored the wisdom of Tola for so many years. He would be more prudent from now.

A great sadness for the village was that there was no trace of the two families that had not been able to return to the village when the great darkness came. Even after the light came back, they found no signs of them. The search party that went to investigate their huts were shocked to find both field-huts destroyed. The thatch roofs and bamboo walls were torn to shreds, and its occupants not to be seen anywhere. It did occur to them that the missing families might have run for shelter to a neighbouring village.

Choba sent out two parties of two men each to the villages closest to them. The men went to inquire if either of the two families had sought shelter in the neighbouring villages, and chosen to remain there. They set out and went from village to village, but no one had any information to give them. One by one, the villages confirmed that not a soul had come seeking refuge to their village during the darktime. Even so, the four villages had many tales to tell of how the darkness had afflicted them. They had also lost people during the darkness, although none of the deaths had been caused by the tiger. They said the people who died were, for the most part, the elderly members, but they were unable to determine if it was simply old age or if it was brought on by the darkness. Since most of them were old and infirm, they would probably have died before the year was out.

One village recounted that it was nightly plagued by sounds of a baby crying. It was not any of the village children; during the night hours, the whimpering would grow louder and louder till it became a shriek. It went on for some days before the seer stopped it with a very powerful spell. He had taken his apprentice with him, and the two men carried wormwood torches and stood at the gate hurling curses at the unquiet spirit. That was the only thing that brought the crying to an end, and after that, the villagers were able to get some rest and sleep.

New dream receivers were revealed in this time. They were duly given their anointing in their respective villages. Some were men, some were women, and all of them used their gifts to help the seer. Only one village had reported being stalked by the giant tiger. It had circled their village and pounded at its walls. But the seer and his father had fastened potent curses on the village walls against spirit attacks, and they had proved just as effective against the tiger.

At least three villages had brought out the *food of war*, and begun using it because they were unsure how long the darkness would last. All of them were witness to the tiger in the sky that regurgitated the sun, before it fell to earth. One village swore the tiger had fallen into a volcanic gorge close to their fields. They said they saw blood spattered on trees near the mouth of the gorge. These and many wondrous accounts they were happy to share. But none of the neighbouring villages had any news of the missing families from *Shumang Laangnyu Sang*.

So, all their searches and queries came to nothing. The search parties confirmed that in the period of the great darkness, not one village had been approached by members of their village seeking sanctuary. In the absence of evidence, it was difficult to say if they had been taken off by predatory animals, or even been abducted by spirits. There were no clues to go on. After their reports were submitted, funeral rituals were performed for the missing members; their houses in the village were shut up until the day of their possible return. If they should show up one day, there would be no question about the ownership of the houses. If they never came back, their houses would be abandoned and left to decay. No one would be allowed to lay an axe to their property and no one would be permitted to occupy the two houses.

The village had to conclude that the tiger had somehow found them and killed them all. No one wanted to harvest the fields of the two households. The two fields were abandoned, and in the winter months when food grew scarce, bears and birds shared the standing grain between themselves. Weeds overtook the lands that man had allowed to fall into neglect. In a few years' time, the furrows returned to wasteland, and people avoided going near the two fields, but would point them out to newcomers and retell all over again the strange, bewildering tale of the tiger that ate the sun.

Chapter Nineteen

For a long time, Namu had maintained that it was Tola who had killed the tiger, not him. But it was true that he had made his village famous by causing the light to come back. When the names of warriors were chanted at festivals, his name would lead the others. Namu was far from pleased. He shied away from the attention and he told this story whenever people tried to heroize him.

'Yes, I did run inside the open mouth of the tiger, but once I was inside, I was snared by a lie. It made me forget my mission, and I lay inside the mouth of the tiger ready to give up everything else beyond the tiger-world. I was that deceived. If it had not been for Grandmother Tola who left her body behind and sent her spirit to call me back, I would not have had the wisdom to kill the tiger.'

His listeners did not know that. What Tola had done was astonishing. Though she said she had seen her father do it once, she herself had never tried it. But she knew it could be done in a great emergency, and for a great purpose. Afterwards, Tola said she would never do it again. But she always insisted that it was only Namu's hand, not hers, that could kill the tiger. If she had tried, she would have failed. She was the message-carrier, the awakener of men to their destinies. To try to be more would be blasphemous, because that was her circumscribed role. Tola would not let them ascribe the honour of saving the village to her.

In her wise way, she said, 'We are not the heroes. There were no heroes here. But we had *Kuneibü nyu*, our mother, the village. Your birth mother is the one you call *Anyu*, but we call the village *Kuneibü nyu*, for she is the mother of us all. Our *Kuneibü nyu* gathered us together in the darkness, she was the one fighting the *Naknyu,* the mother of all darkness, that came to destroy us. *Kuneibü nyu* held us together, giving us her wisdom, and that is how we defeated *Naknyu.*'

For a long time after the killing of the tiger, Namu struggled with his own demons. They came in the dead of night, in his dreams. They came in the daytime too when he was resting between the hard labours of helping widows to repair their houses, or reinforcing the walls of his own house and that of his grandmother's. Whenever his mind was at rest, the images of his father and mother and his two sisters crept in. It made him grow surly and withdraw from Tola and Thongdi. Finally, Tola took him to the gravesite where his parents were buried. The two had been buried together. The bamboo fencing around their graves was now blackened from years of neglect; it would not be replaced, but left to disintegrate and become one with the earth again. Grass had grown over the mounds and the shield of Topong Nyakba, the shield that was customarily propped over a warrior's grave, had rotted away. Tola stopped a few feet from the graves.

'Look! That is where they lie, Topong Nyakba and Sechang. I buried them with my own hands. The widow Sungmo helped me, and so did Beshang. There were no twin daughters buried with them. You alone are the fruit of their brief union. You alone were delivered in your household. The village in the tiger's mouth was a lie, the greatest lie invented to trap you. The family that took you in was a pure lie. The enemy is so powerful because he is able to fabricate the most convincing lies from our infant memories. He knows our past and uses it to destroy our future. If you brood over his lie as you are doing now, you will continue to give it life. Get over that lie before it destroys you because if you do not stop giving it power, it will annihilate you. Stop bringing up those images in your mind. Replace them with truths, the truth of Thongdi's love and devotion for you, and the family you have made with her.'

Tola's firmness was Namu's salvation. She scooped up soil from the grave and placed it in his hand, and he took it and threw it into the woods beyond; it was a cleansing ritual to distance himself from the dead, and in his case, the spirits that impersonated the dead. They turned their backs on the graves of memory, the graves of the dead past and returned home.

The struggle did not stop altogether. The ritual at the grave was just the beginning of a long journey. Namu understood that the dark time had taken a natural desire in him and used it to breed a fantasy that was continuing to work its venom on him. He would stop empowering it as Tola had enjoined; he would close his mind to its entry. In the following days, each time the images returned, as a loving look from Sechang's beautiful face, or the memory of Loni and Noni embracing him, he pushed them away. He stopped hosting them. And as he kept doing that, deliberately closing his mind to the entreaties of the tiger-world, the images fell away, became blurry and indistinct, the sweet voices faded, so that sometimes he went days without thinking of them.

One afternoon, on a day when the village was observing a non-work day, Thongdi was in the inner room, sweeping. She pushed her broom under the bed and used it to pull out the dirt underneath. A round object was caught on the end of her broom. Namu was in the other room when Thongdi gave a small scream. He leapt into the room. 'Thongdi, what is it? Why did you scream?'

Thongdi had covered her mouth with her left hand, her broom was on the floor and she pointed wordlessly to the object on the floor.

'What?' Namu asked as he crept closer to take a look. He recognised the brown ball with ridges down the side. It was the memory ball. Namu was amazed it was still in his possession.

'Is it some animal?' Thongdi asked fearfully. 'I saw it move when my broom swept it out.'

Namu picked it up and carried it in his palm.

'Don't touch it!' Thongdi implored.

'Don't be scared, Thongdi. It's the memory ball that Grandmother Chemden gave me.'

'But isn't that from the tiger-world? Is it alive? Will it bite? Why do you keep it?'

'I really don't know how it got here. Let's go and ask Tola.'

Namu opened Thongdi's hand and placed the memory ball in her palm. It quivered slightly and was still, but Thongdi quickly gave it back to her husband. They showed it to Tola who took the ball and looked at it curiously, and then recognition dawned.

'A memory ball! It's a long time since I have held one. In my childhood, there was a man who had one as a gift from a spirit. He would let my cousins and I borrow it, and we played with it for hours.' She let it roll back and forth on her hand, and counted the ridges on the sides. 'My grandmother used to say that it stores our memories, both good and bad. Only women can be the owners of memory balls. They have the power to acquire them and the right to bestow them as gifts to younger women. I'm surprised that you were given this. Who was the giver again?'

Namu mentioned Chemden's name and that she said she had been waiting to give it to him. Tola smiled when she heard the name.

'Chemden? Ah, how incredible! She was your grandfather's cousin. She died of typhus before the first attack on the village. Of course, it would be Chemden. Did she say how you were to use it?'

'Not really. All she said was that it stores every memory you have made with your loved ones. Oh yes, and that it was a living entity because it is a memory ball of life. But she didn't say more and she seemed anxious for us to leave as it was getting dark.'

'Hmm. Chemden. She was a strange one. At festivals, she served many mugs of brew and set them outside her house, saying the spirits must be given their shares of brew as it was them who gave us our festivals. Everyone suspected she was not quite right in the head. Either that, or, the other explanation is she had access to the other world.'

'But, Grandmother, if the tiger-world was a lie, why has the memory ball travelled into our world?'

'Namu, the only answer I can think of is that while you were in the tiger-world, you also made contact with people who have crossed over. It does happen. Our people say that the truth and the lie travel along the same path until they finally reach the fork that separates them forever. It means the spirits of the dead, and the spirits that are simply personifications of the dead will mingle together before they are separated by the final day of the Creator. Don't be surprised by it. Why would you not have met the spirit of Chemden? And why would you not be vulnerable to spiritual deceit? The world of spirits is a strange world and you are on the path to discovering more about it, Namu. Just remember that we cannot measure it by the experiences of this natural world. You would go very wrong if you tried that.'

Tola gave the memory ball back to Namu. 'Keep it in a safe place, away from the reach of children,' she warned.

Chapter Twenty

In the weeks after the tiger was killed, Tola was stronger than ever. She still appeared stern to an outsider, but the truth was that she felt like a different person, light-hearted and unburdened. The tiger was killed, their village had fulfilled the destiny that her father had prophesied so many years ago, the same destiny her nocturnal visitor had pointed her to in the visitations. Surely now that the spirit tiger had been killed, and the light retrieved by that action, surely the visits had stopped for good. That was what Tola hoped. But a month after the tiger was killed, the visitor returned for one last time.

It was in the dead of night. The village was asleep, the ever-vigilant dogs had stopped barking, and the rooster would not crow for some hours. Tola was dreaming of her father. He wore a thick, dark body-cloth, the kind that only seers wore and he was walking away from her. 'Father! Wait for me!' Tola shouted to the retreating figure, but her father walked on as though he had not heard her. He kept walking in the direction of the hill they called the valley of souls. All seers agreed it was the first destination of dead souls, before they journeyed on to the next world. Her feet were heavy as lead as she half crawled and half dragged herself after him before he disappeared at the bend in the road. Tola stretched out her hands in a vain attempt to stop him, and cried despairingly, 'Father!' before waking up sweating.

Tears were running down her cheeks and the dream was so real that she continued to whimper and cry for some time. The door of her house being pushed open startled her into wakefulness. The visitor walked in soundlessly and stood by the end of her bed. A muffled scream escaped her before he put his finger to her mouth and paralysed all speech. As before, he was dressed as a warrior, his resplendent headdress grazing the main beam of the house. He stood at the foot of her bed, stony-faced and unsmiling. If his manner were less magisterial, he would have appeared handsome. As it was, Tola was always overwhelmed by his regal presence to register anything else.

Still, she struggled and she gesticulated as she tried to say the words, 'Why do you return now? Have I not done what you asked me to do? You can see I am very old. Leave me be. Let me live the rest of my days in peace.' She need not have worried that she could not utter these thoughts. The visitor sensed her distress and her confusion, and each of her thoughts were transparent to him.

'Tola, your mission is not finished yet,' he began. 'You are to help Namu to live out his destiny. Stop protesting. Just listen carefully. I will tell you why and how. Namu is the chosen one. Life has been preparing him. But Namu will try to avoid it vehemently. This is always the case with greatness. Those destined to be great will do anything to avoid it. They will become content with the ordinariness of daily life – a wife and children, a field and a good harvest each year, and their turn at the drum two or three times a year. They will crave nothing more, least of all will they want to save villages, and men, with their gifts. The great disaster of your day is over. But a village that disregards or forgets the wisdom of its ancestors becomes a village deprived of weapons to fight threats in the future.

'I am talking about the manner in which *Shumang Laangnyu Sang* learned to stay strong and keep faith and prepare the way for the spirit tiger to be destroyed. The future generations must always know how their elders conquered their enemies, so that they can use the same wisdom when their turn comes. Repeat the stories to them in every generation. Namu is to be the knowledge bearer and the faith keeper of his generation. The past is to be used to prepare the future. But the future is always more important than the past. Teach him that clearly. He has to show others that the only way to walk into a strong future is to leave the past behind; and he has to start with himself.

'But remember, not every man will be given the honour of a great destiny. Namu is one. It may not appear in his children's generation, yet possibly it may reappear in that of his grandchildren. That is how it goes. Tola, you need to pass on all you have learned to him. Tell it to him, tell him everything. Don't hold back a thing. Teach him to receive. Help him use his faith to access knowledge. You owe this to your father and the line of seers to which you too belong.'

The visitor turned to go, but Tola quickly detained him with her words, 'And if he refuses his destiny, what do I do then?'

'If you hide nothing from him, he will not refuse. Don't you remember when he was young, how eagerly he would listen to you. Namu has the qualities required of greatness: he has a teachable heart. He will listen, he will learn. He has a listening heart.'

Then he was gone. That was the last Tola saw of her nocturnal visitor. She continued to lie on her back in bed, exhausted. Then, as she had done before, she slowly went through everything he had told her. The same sense of urgency which she felt after his visits returned to her. Tola peeped out the window. It was pitch dark. There was nothing unusual about this darkness as it was the middle of the night and the stillness would abide for some hours. But for Tola, all sleep had been chased away by the visitation. She slowly got up and lit the fire, keeping it low to avoid waking any of the other inmates. She put the kettle over the flames and waited for it to boil. There were some tea leaves in her tea box, and she measured a spoonful into a blackened enamel mug. When the water boiled, she poured it into the mug and waited. The swirling tea leaves finally settled at the bottom of the mug, and Tola slowly poured the tea into a well-used cup.

Ever since Namu and Thongdi had moved into her house during the dark time, they had stayed put. They insisted that Tola was too old to be living on her own. They said they wanted to take care of her if she fell ill. 'At least if we are in the same house, I can make you soup in no time at all,' Thongdi said. Tola had smiled and agreed with the young ones. If they wanted to live under her roof, who was she to object to that arrangement?

While they slept on, she slowly finished her tea and began to make more hot water. There was no moon, she knew that as she had checked earlier. The moonless nights reminded her of the dark time and she never liked to stand outside, as others did, peering at the night skies, looking for stars or warrior souls journeying home.

Tola made a second cup of tea, and between sips she repeated to herself what the visitor had said. She repeated it two or three times so that she would not forget anything. It was still very dark outside and waiting for the others to wake up made her back ache. Tola went to her bed and lay down, but she did not pull her bedclothes over herself, not wanting the warmth to lull her

Chapter Twenty-one

Chongshen's daughter-in-law was also pregnant. The two women, Thongdi and Asonla, became pregnant around the same time, but Thongdi was much bigger than the other woman. Thongdi had just completed six months, but her stomach was so big that people would stop to ask if her time was already at hand. Their questions frightened Thongdi and she wondered if something unusual could have happened to her during the dark time. But Namu had a dream where Thongdi's grandmother came to them, bringing two piglets. The squealing piglets were pink and healthy and blemish-free. The next night, he dreamed that the grandmother returned with a gift of two excellent gourds. Both gourds were the same size and it was difficult to tell them apart. He confided these dreams to Tola because he did not know what it meant. 'Of course, it might not be anything,' he began to say.

Tola fixed her eye sternly on him. 'Never let such words come out of you, Namumolo,' she scolded. 'You are not like other men. Your dreams are truths for yourself or for others. These dreams are simple enough to interpret. What does it mean in the natural world when the spirit world gives you two of everything? What else? Your wife will bear twin daughters or sons. The blessings of your household will be double that of others.'

'Ah Grandmother, you must be right. Thongdi is so much bigger than Asonla that she feared something abnormal had happened to her.'

'Calm her fears. Nothing is wrong except that her womb has been enlarged to make space for the greater blessing she will receive.'

Namu smiled broadly at the interpretation to his dream.

'I wish I were half as wise as you, Grandmother.'

Tola did not return his smile. 'Then use your heart to listen. It is more important now than ever that you learn to do that,' she said in her dead serious manner.

The half-smile on Namu's face faded. 'What do you mean by that, Grandmother?'

'Namu, you are going to be a father soon. Thongdi will give birth in two and a half or three months to twins. That is an enormous responsibility. But there is more awaiting you. You have had a taste of what it is to be a seer. Even though the duration was not long, you were seer over men's destinies during the dark time. There is a time coming when you will be called to the same role for the village. A seer is a dream-receiver. You are already becoming a dream-receiver. There will be more profound dreams; there will be dreams for the village, and you must grow into the wisdom of reading those dreams accurately.'

'But Grandmother, isn't that part of my life already over? I have killed the spirit tiger as you trained me to, and my friends cut off all its six evil tails. Haven't I done my duty by the village?'

'That is only the beginning, Namu. There is more coming.'

'More coming?' He looked troubled at this information. 'There is a part of me that wants to listen to everything, Grandmother.

But part of me is reluctant to know more. My heart is restless.' Namu lowered his voice.

'And Grandmother,' he continued, 'I don't want to be seer. That is too big a responsibility. Even if the blood of seers runs in our family, can they not find someone older to be seer? Maybe get someone from another village in the same clan as ours. Seers cannot leave the village borders for fear the virtue of the village would be taken away. Seers should have the answers to all kinds of calamities or at least, they should have the means to get answers if a calamity of any sort happens. I am not ready to take on that responsibility.'

Tola left it at that. She would not be the one to persuade him; it would not be right. Let the men come. It was their responsibility, not hers. She might be the oldest member of the village and the daughter of seers; that did not mean she had any right to violate the protocol of seer hunting.

They didn't have to wait long. Two days later, Choba and Chongshen visited them.

'Aunt, are you well?' They both called out when they saw Tola sitting by the fire. Tola, in turn replied that she was so well that she suspected she was going into her second youth. They spoke in this light manner to each other, and she bade them sit by her.

'Is Namu home?' Choba asked and before she could answer, Namu walked in the door and stood before them, welcoming them to the house. Thongdi began to put the kettle on the fire to prepare black tea for the visitors.

'How are you Namu? Not too tired from feasting with your age-mates?' Namu's mates had been celebrating a small mid-year festival for warriors. He assured them that the feasting had gone smoothly.

'Did you get the cut in your leg looked at?'

'I am very well, dear uncles. The cut was not deep at all. It healed in two days.' Namu was referring to a cut he had received from his own spear point when he was sharpening it some mornings ago. 'I used some Crofton weed on it, and every morning I covered it with rock bee honey until the cut closed. Look it's completely healed now.'

'It's good that you are acquainting yourself with native medicines. In future, many will come to you to ask for cures, so your herbal education should be extensive.'

Namu looked at the two men a bit suspiciously. His eyes darted from one to the other. 'Why would others seek me out? I am an ordinary householder possessing the same amount of knowledge they also have. They could use their own cures.'

Choba looked askance at Chongshen, and indicated that he was to begin.

'Namu, we are here to ask you to be seer for the village.' Chongshen had not bothered with a preface. He was not a tactful man, and chose to state the case directly. Namu rose to his feet, and stood there looking at the three of them – Choba, Chongshen and Tola.

'Did I hear right, Uncles? You want me to be seer?' Namu's voice was deliberately low, as though he did not want the neighbours to hear.

'That is right, Namu,' replied Choba. 'Your great-grandfather was seer. Your father would have been seer but he died prematurely. And you are now a grown man. You understand partially what it is to occupy this position. We come to ask you to be seer, Namumolo. You know this is a formality. You are the rightful seer, not Chongshen.'

Namu hung his head, and blurted out, 'I am not ready, I am not ready yet.'

'No one is ever ready. But life waits for very few people, my son,' Choba continued in a softer tone. 'Take some days to think about it. Listen to your dreams. Listen to your heart.' The men left while Namu continued to sit where he was, covering his head with his hands.

Chapter Twenty-two

Namu remained in that position long after the men had left. Finally, he spoke.

'Grandmother, tell them I do not want to be seer.'

Tola was harsh with him. 'You are no longer a boy, Namu. You cannot hide behind me anymore.'

'But you don't understand, any of you. I don't want to be a leader. I have done my part. I killed the spirit tiger. And whatever preparation I made in killing him came from you, not from myself, for I have no wisdom. All I want in my life is to live in peace with my neighbours, farm our fields and be able to look after you and Thongdi and my children. What man would want more than that out of life? Only a fool...' He didn't finish his sentence.

Tola did not say anything. She was shocked to see the prophecy fulfilment taking place in front of her very eyes, in her hearing. She cast about for the right words to speak to the obstinacy of Namu's heart. But she failed to find any, and her next sentence was delivered in a more subdued tone.

'Let your dreams guide you, as they said. See if you will have more dreams, and if you do, be led well by them.' She rose from her chair and went out, Thongdi following close behind her. The women did not look at each other, but when Tola sat down on the sunlit porch, Thongdi combed her silver hair and massaged Tola's scalp. It was her way of comforting the older woman. Thongdi divided Tola's long hair and started to braid it into a single plait at the back.

'He is afraid,' Thongdi whispered, while weaving her fingers through the old woman's hair.

'Pray he will get a dream to lead him,' Tola whispered back.

The women kept sitting outside on the porch, out of his way. Very shortly after, Namu left for the forest with a dao and a cane basket. He was vague about what he was going to do.

'I'll see if I can get some good wood,' he mumbled before he left.

The rainy season was in full spate. This was no time to cut wood for any purpose. But neither of the women said anything, and he walked swiftly away from the house and village, as though he wanted to avoid answering any more questions. Namu soon walked into a storm and had to take shelter in a field shed. In these days, rain-soaked clouds would empty their burdens without warning, and in moments, heavy rain would flood the fields so they stayed water-logged for weeks. The roof of the shed he was sheltering in was hopeless; the owner had not had time to put new thatch before the dark time descended. It looked like he still had not found the time now. The rain was merciless, it came in through the leaky roof soaking him to the skin and dripping from the bag he carried. Namu crouched in the shed hiding away from his family, hiding from members of the village, hiding from himself, and he watched the rain beat down on the vegetation.

Why would they not let him alone? Why were they insisting on making him seer? All he wanted in life was to be a good husband and a good father, when the time came. He sat there feeling sorry for himself, waiting for the rain to ease up so he could go on his way.

But it rained the whole afternoon and Namu tired of waiting so he walked into the rain, letting it soak again the clothes that had not dried when he was sheltering in the shed. He walked aimlessly into the forest, away from the fields until he lost his bearings. Evening was closing in, and he desperately looked for shelter; he saw the lights of a village in the distance, and he made his way to it until the path led him to the foot of the mount of Mvüphri.

By the time Namu reached the village of Mvüphri, it had grown quite dark. The gate was mercifully still open, and he ran inside and found the village square. Strangers who had no shelter for the night could stand at the village square until someone came by to host them. Namu was the only one at the square; if there were other travellers to Mvüphri that day, they must have been given shelter before he arrived at the village. He stood there worrying that he might be overlooked, but soon, a small man ran over and called out, 'Follow me!' He led Namu to a very big house beside the village square, and Namu realised it was the house of the seer.

'Welcome, Namumolo. You are a long way from home, and should not risk travelling back. You may spend the night here in our house.' Namu's host looked very pleased to see him. A tall, authoritative man, the seer of Mvüphri was known for his hospitality. In the neighbouring villages, word had spread that the seer of Mvüphri had such abundant harvests that he sought every opportunity to host travellers and use the grain to feed them. The act multiplied their grain in their granaries, and the more they gave away, the more was added to them. Their cattle birthed in all seasons, and mealtimes at the seer's house was like a small festival, with crowded tables where the poor came to eat and be filled.

'Have you eaten, Namumolo?' the seer asked solicitously. It surprised Namu very much that they knew his name in these parts. It was his first time in Mvüphri, and he could only suppose they had heard the story of the tiger-killing, else how would they know who he was?

'No, Seer, I have not eaten. I lost my way when it rained, and it was too late to turn so I followed the lights and came to your village.'

'We have dinner ready – you can join us.' The seer led Namu inside the house to a great kitchen. There were about four fire-places where pots of meat and rice were cooking. Two women served them food as soon as they sat down at the long table. The aroma of meat cooked with country ginger and dried red chilli wafted upward. Steaming plates of rice were set before them, and a young girl brought a bowl of green vegetables, and it was she who served them throughout.

Namu was astonished at the amount of food available at dinner. 'Is there a festival going on or do you always eat like this?'

'Well, you see, Namu, the cook knows exactly how many people are to be expected so he cooks food accordingly. None of this food ever goes to waste, and it may seem luxurious to you, but believe me, everyone who needs it is fed by it, and at the end of the day, there are no leftovers.'

'That is rather unbelievable,' Namu exclaimed, as he tried to wrap his head around the information.

There were other people eating on the far side of the table. A young mother and her four hungry children were devouring the food in front of them. They came to thank the seer saying they had not eaten so well in the past two months.

'What happened?' asked the seer.

'Our grain finished during the dark time and the grain in the fields were damaged beyond restoration. We have been starving.'

'From today, you may eat here every day until you can work your fields again.' The woman was very grateful as she had lost her husband the previous year.

When the diners had left one by one, the seer turned his full attention on Namu.

'Well young Namu, I hear that you do not want to be seer.' The seer of Mvüphri did not smile when he posed this question. Namu made haste to answer,

'It is not that I don't want to be seer. I am not ready. I am still too young.'

'There is not a single time when one is completely ready. If we reached such a time, we would be dead, as we are nearest perfection when we are about to die.'

Namu was startled by this answer. How powerful the seer of Mvüphri must be to know all that he knew about Namu, mainly his unwillingness to be seer.

'What did you learn when you killed the spirit-tiger?'

The question came so unexpectedly that Namu had no time to reflect on his answer. 'I was overwhelmed with the sense of freedom. And the next thing was I felt overwhelmed at the pure happiness that comes from helping others.'

Namu hoped he had not sounded too sentimental.

'What a beautiful definition – the pure happiness that comes from having helped others. That is what I would say seership is. Do you still not think it is worth seeking?'

Namu did not need to answer him. His doubts were clearing up. The seer saw that and added, 'Go home tomorrow. Listen to what your grandmother has to tell you. You don't need my counsel when Tola holds the key to the questions in your heart.'

Namu slept very well in the bed they gave him. In the morning, he thanked his host and set off for *Shumang Laangnyu Sang*.

And because Namu had the humility of the listening heart, the ability to learn from his elders, he grew in strength and wisdom.

Chapter
Twenty-three

' I am grateful we have finished all field work for this year. In my present condition I wouldn't be able to do any work even if I managed to get to the field.' Thongdi moved with great difficulty now as she was in her ninth month. Her older sister came to help from time to time. Even simple things like taking a bath had to be done with her sitting on a stool and her sister pouring water over her after she finished soaping herself. She wouldn't allow Namu to help her. He was seer now and had more important things to think about such as the spiritual welfare of the whole village.

On the morning of the birth, severe labour pains woke Thongdi up. The summer months were past, but the rain was still with them. Out of the window she saw that the skies were overcast and the fog was moving down toward the village. She drank her tea quickly and set a pot of rice on the fire. But her pains were on the increase and she allowed her sister to take over the cooking. A young boy had been sent to fetch the midwife. She came from the next village as their village midwife had died shortly after the dark time. The village women had quickly arranged for a younger woman to be trained to take on the job of assisting at birthings. There had been no delay. A midwife was as essential to a village as a seer. Births went on at all times; birthing could happen in the middle of a war, a festival, a harvest, even a death. Such was life. Birthing was life usurping death, over and over. Agricultural societies celebrated births eagerly and welcomed the extra hands that would eventually join the family at cultivating rice.

The midwife knew her job well. She had a pleasant bedside manner, and was diligent about washing her hands each time she examined the patient. Thongdi had tried slowly walking round the interior of the house, but when the labour pains escalated, her knees buckled beneath her. They partially carried her to the bed and she lay on her side, sweat running down her neck from the intensity of the pain. Her back felt as though it would break, while her distended stomach would not be satisfied in any position. The contractions returned with unfailing regularity, each time leaving her gasping for breath. She pushed away the midwife's hands on her lower abdomen, but the woman soothed her saying, 'Not long at all now, my dear, not long.'

The midwife began to give her instructions without stopping. *Don't cry out, it will waste your energy. Concentrate,* she urged, *concentrate on pushing every time you feel the urge to push. Here, drink some soup, it will give you strength.* Between encouraging the exhausted woman, feeding her soup, wiping her forehead and pressing her back, the midwife expertly caught the first baby as it slid its way out into the world. She quickly passed it to Thongdi's mother, and turned her attention back to Thongdi. The second baby did not wait; a wet little head emerged and it was gently persuaded to leave its first home for a brighter second home.

Pandemonium broke out as both babies began to howl. But the midwife had had years of experience. She made Namu sit on a cane morra and carry the second baby while she attended to Thongdi and made sure the afterbirth was expelled. She fed her more soup, adjusted her pillow and only then did she turn her attention to the new-borns.

The two little girls had healthy lungs. Thongdi's mother fed them warm water from a cup, and laughed as they greedily tried to suckle the spoon. Thongdi's sister prepared bath water for the babies, and brought out the flannel cloths that Thongdi had kept ready. The midwife bathed the older one first and marvelled at how thick her hair was. The baby gripped her thumb and would not let it go. Easing out of its grip, the midwife made more warm water, and took the second baby from its father. As the midwife washed away the thick mucus that covered the baby, she started to scream.

'What is it?' Thongdi asked. 'Are they dead? What's happening?' Her screams brought Tola to the entrance of the room.

The midwife calmed herself and lifted the baby to the light so the others could get a look at her. The baby had milky white skin and snow-white hair, whiter than Tola's hair. Gasps were heard around the room.

'Grandmother!' That was all Namu could say.

Tola quickly came to the middle of the room. 'Don't be alarmed,' she said. 'This is yet another rare blessing. Namu, Thongdi, your children have gone through the dark time and survived. They are carrying the marks of that experience on their bodies. The first one is Night, summer-night haired and dark as a berry that has been lying in the sun. The second one is Day, the pale colour of day after the darkness lifted. No wonder she is so white and looks bloodless. But don't worry. They are the creator's work so we might never forget the story of the dark time.'

'So there is nothing wrong with her? We don't need to take her to the forest?' Namu's voice stammered at the second question. He was asking if he should take the baby to the forest and abandon it to avert any curse that it could bring to the village.

'The baby carries no curse. It is a channel of blessing. Don't take the counsel of the foolish. They fear anything that is different. But you, Namu, will lead the way in embracing the extraordinary. For that is the way to further wisdom.'

The midwife resumed cleaning the second baby. Her skin was translucent, they could almost see the blood running through her thin veins. She was truly beautiful.

Tola instructed Namu to hang out leaves at the entrance of their house in a prominent place to discourage visitors. When people saw it, they would understand that the household was undergoing the period of purification rituals for the new mother. Most visitors would then postpone their business to a future time when the leaves would be taken down by the home owners.

There was always a lot to be done after a birth. Naming of the new-borns, was, of course, the most urgent activity, and this would be done in the next two days. Thongdi was served food before any of the other members of the house. Chicken soup, cocoyam broth and the occasional treat of sticky rice pancakes. In the days that followed, they were all kept fully occupied with the twins who were quite demanding and disrespectful of the scrupulous routine the home had followed before their entry. At the end of the day, the grown-ups in the house were fatigued and slept as soon as they fell into bed.

Chapter Twenty-four

Tola turned in bed and found a position where her back did not hurt. She was what she called bone-weary. Sleep came immediately. But her sleep was disturbed by dreams of her father. She could see him, but as in the earlier dreams, he was very far off and she was too tired to try and reach him.

'Tola, it's Sungmo!' A hand began to shake her awake. Every cell in her body craved rest and sleep, and she ignored the hand on her shoulder. 'Come on Tola, you have to come and see this,' the voice insisted.

With great difficulty, Tola prised her eyes open. A smiling Sungmo was waiting at the foot of her bed, her hand stretched out to her. In the next moment, Tola was wide awake and she got out of bed to follow Sungmo out the door. What marvellous thing was Sungmo going to show her? Tola wondered as they came to the village square. The square was overflowing with people. What had happened? How come she was not aware there would be a gathering of the village? Did Namu not know of this? No one had told them anything. Perhaps they had come and hesitated at the door on seeing the leaves.

Fascinated, she followed Sungmo around the square. An elderly man was standing at the centre; he wore a colourful cloth with wide red bands bordered by black stripes. A wealthy man's cloth. He raised his hand in greeting, and he smiled as though something had deeply amused him. Tola went toward him. It couldn't be, but it was! It was her father. 'Father! I was trying so hard to catch up with you, but you didn't hear me calling you!' Tola exclaimed as she caught hold of him, determined not to let him out of her sight this time. He gave her an indulgent smile, as if to say he would not leave her again.

Tola looked at the people around them, not sure she could recognise the smiling faces. A man much younger than her father broke away from a group of people and approached her. He came striding towards her and Tola looked behind her to see if he was looking for someone else. But there was no one. The man came right up to her and, with a little shock, Tola realised it was her husband. 'No! Is it really you?' A little gasp escaped her as he caught her hands in his. It was indeed her husband, father of Topong Nyakba, her beloved husband who had refused to put her away. He looked the same as he had on the first day of their marriage. His skin was smooth as a baby's and Tola could not see any burn scars on him; no one would know he had died in a fire that charred him and his friends beyond recognition. Tola looked at him again, unable to comprehend it. 'Look at you!' she exclaimed, 'how well you look!'

'No.' He smiled. 'Look at you, how radiant you are!' Tola laughed at the idea. And she raised her hands to show him how wrinkled they were, but they were as unlined as a young woman's. However, there was no time to ponder over what had happened. Sungmo had returned looking as though she was in a hurry. Beshang was at the back of her, and he beamed when he saw Tola.

'You have to come this way. You won't believe it,' Sungmo said and Tola followed her without a second thought. Beyond the square, there stood a village, slightly smaller than the present village. The houses were built in a much more traditional manner with thatch roofs and split bamboo walls secured with twine. The houses had been constructed in a straight line on either side and were so close to each other, there was almost no space between the houses.

'Where have you taken me, Sungmo?'

'Do you not see?'

Tola looked again, and understood why it was so familiar. It was the village of her childhood. She broke into a run. Her legs no longer dragged after her. She ran until she reached a house she knew so well she could have found it blindfolded. Her mother was sitting inside, the light from a window falling on her hair. 'Mother! I thought I would never see you again!' Tola embraced her mother and tears came to her eyes.

'Hush, my child, no one cries here. We have left tears behind us,' her mother soothed her.

'I'm just shedding happy tears,' Tola tried to explain.

'Come my dear,' her mother called to her. Holding hands, they walked out of the house.

The village was the old village, the one that existed before the attack. Every way she turned, there was a familiar face, a neighbour, a cousin, an aunt, everyone wanted to greet her. 'How we have been waiting for you, Tola,' some of them said, as they welcomed her. A male cousin came up to her and teased, 'You took so long to get here, what happened?' He laughed in a conspiratorial manner, and she understood that she need not explain anything. Tola looked and looked around her, and it truly was the village of her childhood. What magic had Sungmo worked? How had it been possible to resurrect a village that was destroyed by enemy warriors? Yet every time the question rose up her throat, another loved one would come before her, and greet her, and she never found time to ask Sungmo.

Topong Nyakba and Sechang came and stood before her. Shyly they greeted her, 'Do you remember us, Mother?'

'Oh my dear ones, how I have longed for this.' Tola held them both. They looked at each other for a long time, and embraced again. Where was Sungmo? She really must ask her if she could stay. Tola turned away from the crowds of people to look for Sungmo. It was then she saw her own house and the open door. Namu and Thongdi and the babies. They were still sleeping. She felt torn between the two worlds. They needed her – how could she go now?

Sungmo was at her side.

'It's your time, Tola. Don't worry about them. They are young, they will manage. You have done much for them. Let go of them now. Can you not see how the others are waiting for you?'

Everything Sungmo was saying was true. Tola remembered how young and strong Thongdi was, and she had her sister and mother to help her. And Namu? Tears filled her eyes at the thought of Namu. But Namu would have to learn to fully step into manhood. She had carried him long enough on her back. Perhaps she would stunt his growth if she chose to stay behind. It was good for him to learn to walk on his own.

'Namumolo will be stronger than ever, don't you worry,' Sungmo said.

Tola turned and followed Sungmo into her father's house.

Glossary of native words and place names

Morung: a large hall used as a community centre. The Morung is a multi-purpose institution. It functions like a training area for different age groups of young men where they are taught their role in the community, and the different roles they will occupy. They learn the stories of the tribe and strategies of war. At the morung they learn to work hard at fetching firewood, or cleaning the morung and obeying one's elders. Czech researcher Milada Ganguli describes the morung as 'a centre for social interaction and institution for handing down tradition to the younger generations.'

Age-group: Some researchers describe the age-group as a work-force of young people born within three years of each other. It is common to have such groups in the community where the members come together and work in each other's fields or work on some other projects. Marriage partners are generally found within the same age-group. Festivals and big events are celebrated by age-group members together. The age-group works as a smart way of estimating a person's age and the knowledge he/she would have accrued at that age.

Genna-day: A genna day is a no-work day for several reasons which are announced by the headman. If some members of the village have died by drowning or in a fire or some accident occurring beyond the village, a genna day is observed. No one goes to the fields on a genna day. Some other reasons for observing a genna-day are – solar eclipse, earthquakes, extreme weather, and calamities visiting the village. It is held to propitiate the spirits and to prevent future accidents of the same nature recurring.

Taboo: Many of the Naga cultures are guided by taboos. There are marriage taboos deciding which villages may not intermarry. Common taboo actions are: stealing, lying, cheating, deceiving a host or a parent, desecrating sacred places, being arrogant etc.

Log drum: The log drum is the largest musical instrument of the Naga tribes. Its use is restricted to certain tribes such as the Chang, Konyak, Khiamniungan, Ao Phom, Sangtam and Yimchungrü. The log drum is multipurpose and used for communicating dangers such as invasions, fires or natural predators. to villagers. Each warning is given with different rhythmic beats. At festivals, a different rhythm is used. The drum is made out of a single tree, and its inside is hewn out making it light to carry. Myanmarese San Lin Tun, freelance writer, documents that the work of hewing out the drum and carving it takes about ten days, and it is 'a central part of the spiritual and cultural life' of the Nagas. During a lunar eclipse, men beat the drum and shout, 'release our moon, release our moon' because they believe the moon is being eaten by a tiger or a frog.

The great log-drum of Aliba village is recorded as measuring 36 feet in length and 6.8 feet in diameter, about 21.37 feet in circumference. It took about 39 days to uproot the tree and carve it, and 36 days to drag it from the forest to the village, a distance of 3.33 kilometres. The log drum was dragged to the village in Spring, 1981, under the leadership of the Medemsanger putu (council).

Jhum: Jhum is the term used in Northeast India to refer to the slash and burn method of rice cultivation.

Body-cloth: a wide piece of woven cloth that can cover a man's body. Both men and women wear body-cloths. Each tribe has its distinctive pattern on its body-cloth.

Waist-cloth: a waist-cloth is a woman's garment. Smaller and narrower than the body-cloth, it can be tied around the waist like a sarong.

Creator deity: the deity worshipped by all the Naga tribes, and recognised as the creator of heaven and earth. It is a male deity and considerably mightier than the spirits that are always in conflict with man. The creator deity is a noble and ethical figure, worshipped at festivals and at every great event in a man's life.

Great-roofed houses: These are houses with jutting roofs of a very distinctive architecture. The only people in the village who own great-roofed houses are men of title who have given feasts for the whole village. Under the jutting roofs, the skulls of the animals killed to host the village are hung in rows.

Anyu: Mother, language: Chang
Abi Nyu: Grandmother, language: Chang
Shambulee: God, or our Creator, language: Chang
Kuneibü nyu: our mother, language: Chang

Place names

Shumang Laangnyu Sang: River Rock village. It is the central village in the story. Shumang means river, Laangnyu means rock and Sang means village in the Chang language. The village gets its name for two reasons. The first is its geographical location beside a rocky range through which a river flowed. The fields of the village are irrigated by the tributaries of the river. The other meaning of the River Rock village is the headman's explanation that they were going to be a village with a rock-solid foundation that would be sought by others who needed the untainted wisdom their seers could offer like clear river water.

Mvüphri: imaginary village named after the mountain below which it is built. In the story, it stands for clarity and integrity. As a literary device, it helps to remove the seer from the action of the story so it can progress without his intervention. Mvüphri's gift is self-awareness and the seer of Shumang Laangnyu returns a changed man. He readily admits his deceit of the village when he was seer.

Aliba: A village of the Ao tribe with more than 250 households. Aliba is famed for its magnificent log drum. The beating of the drum can be heard in several neighbouring villages such as, Longkhum, Mangmetong, Khensa and even the villages of the Changki. The villages of the Ao tribe are neighbours to the Chang tribe.

Longkhum: Famous village of the Ao tribe, about 13.6 kilometres from Aliba. The legend of Longkhum says that if you visit the village once, you have to visit it again because your spirit stays behind on the first visit.

Mangmetong: A large Ao village with more than 770 houses. It is 10.6 kilometres from Aliba.

Khensa: Khensa is considered a village of medium size with around 426 families. It is an Ao village about 9.8 kilometres from Aliba.

Changki: Changki village does not have any log drums. There is a story that in the past they had a log drum, but people did not look after it properly causing the log drum to be so offended that it rolled away from the village, and never came back again.

Dark time accounts

The Rengma village of Tseminyu has some of the most unusual origin and settling stories. The village headman is convinced that the village of Tseminyu was settled more than two thousand years ago.

A powerful origin story told and retold by the villagers is an oral account handed down by their forefathers: One day when all the villagers were out in their fields, a thick darkness suddenly covered the land. It came without any warning; it was a very unusual darkness, quite different from a solar eclipse which people referred to as the dying of the sun. It was the middle of the day, but the darkness was so pervasive the people abandoned their work and ran home to the village. Everyone wondered what had caused the darkness, and when they reached home, they enquired of the seer. He explained that the unnatural darkness had been caused because something terrible happened on that day. God had one son; his name was Metishu. God had only this one son and he loved him very dearly. Metishu was a very good and obedient boy, and very loving. Everyone liked him. But on that very afternoon, Metishu, the son of God was killed, and his father was so sad that he covered the whole earth with darkness. That was the dark time that came to our village.

The second dark time story is from the Chang tribe.

Many years ago, an inexplicable darkness fell upon the Chang villages and people were confused and sad and fearful. The darkness lasted several days and no one could come out of their houses as it was too dangerous. One afternoon, while people were locked inside their houses, a man heard a terrible noise. He took his spear and ran out to investigate the source of the noise. It came from a tiger that was sitting on his neighbour's roof, getting ready to pounce. The man quickly fetched his bow and arrows and shot at the animal. The arrow found its mark and the tiger roared and fell off the roof as he died. All the people came out of their houses when they heard the tiger had been killed. Together they found the six tails of the tiger and made sure to cut off all six tails. After that action, the light rapidly returned to the village and they were all saved. Some accounts of the Chang story say the tiger had two tails and some claim it had six tails.

The tribe established a major festival called Naknyulum to commemorate the return of the light. Naknyu means mother of all darkness, lum means festival. Every year this festival is celebrated by the Chang people. The tribe celebrates the triumph of good over evil.

The third Dark time account is from a letter written by Tiberius to Pontius Pilate:

'What I want to ask you about is the mysterious celestial incident that occurred on Friday afternoon after the month of April. A thick darkness moved towards us coming from the South eastern horizon of the Mediterranean Sea and darkened our skies for several hours.' This letter is documented by Dr Paul Maier, in his book *Pontius Pilate* where he also records the reply of Pontius Pilate to Tiberius: 'Regarding the darkness, it indeed covered all of Judah during the indicated time. However, the local astrologer simply can't explain it. The darkness was accompanied by an earthquake. Still the darkness continues to be a complete mystery.' (Dr Paul Maier p 244).

NAKNYULUM – the Festival of Light

The major festival of the Chang tribe is a celebration of light coming to dispel the great darkness. It is quite different from the main festivals of all the other Naga tribes as it is not dictated by the agricultural cycle. There are no satisfactory accounts to explain the sudden transformation of day into night in a period of Chang history. The Changs say the light suddenly vanished and the world was plunged into darkness. For six days and six nights the murkiness remained. Life came to a complete halt and it was a difficult time as it was not possible for folk to carry out their daily activities. It was impossible for people to go to the fields, or go hunting or foraging for food; they could not fetch water, or pound grain, or chop firewood or collect wood in the forest. Even the little firewood they had stacked turned damp and mouldy, and moss and fungi sprouted on the wood. People grew so desperate that they dismantled the beams and posts from their houses, and burned them for light and warmth. Only the rich could keep their home fires burning by using as fuel the many heads of cattle that were on display on the walls.

In this period of darkness, people starved and grew sick; they became depressed with the hopelessness of their situation. But there was a brave warrior named *Namumulou* who refused to submit to the unyielding gloom. He could hear the moaning of his people, and their sorrowful cries all around him as he sat in his house, sharpening all the points of his arrows by the dim light of a bamboo torch. "What is happening"? he wondered. "What is this power throwing this great shadow over us?"

On the sixth night when all his arrows were sharpened, *Namumulou* took his bow and bent it so he could tighten the string and keep it ready. He then stepped outside into the blackness. As his eyes became accustomed to the dark, he could discern a great shadowy figure looming over the rooftops. Choosing a good position, he raised his crossbow and shot arrow after arrow at the ominous shadow until at last, the figure fell to the ground. In that instant, the darkness lifted and the light suddenly returned. To this day, the Chang people celebrate the festival of Naknyulum with all its accompanying rituals to commemorate the coming of the light into a dark world.

The story continues with *Namumulou* going closer to investigate what his arrows had found as target. It was a huge tiger. But it was no ordinary tiger, for it had six long tails. *Namumulou* cut off the tiger's six tails, and remarking that it was something the world had never seen before, he hung them up on a tree. He proceeded to skin the tiger, all the while saying that it was something the world had never seen before, and he draped the tiger skin on a large rock. Till today, the rock is to be seen bearing the impression of the tiger skin, and though the tree upon which the tiger tails were hung has long decayed and died, another tree of the same family has grown up in its place. Ever since that night when that extraordinary tiger with its six tails was shot down and the light returned to the world, the Chang people have observed the counting of the month every year to usher in Naknyulum while abiding by all the rituals of its celebration.

When *Muonglit*, or July, the seven month of the year arrives, people are aware that Naknyulum will soon be celebrated. All members of the tribe make a commitment to rid their houses of diseases and pestilence. One of the first rituals is to cut a lean *Aobu* tree. A decorative ball is woven with some of the twine.

The *Aobu* tree is placed in the Morung and the decorative ball is hung on the tree by a long rope. This takes place in July and at this time, women walk through the village and chant in unison, "*Ho, ho nanuba to namak saa-maa yeiso yangso.*" They address all the breastfeeding mothers saying, "All breastfeeding mothers, we can smell the feed." Another group of women walks about chanting, "*Ojeb pala wangji-phake maitei lemang küyang monyü monyü*" which means, "May the winds sweep away all sickness and hardships from our village."

Then in the eighth month *Naklit*, or August, when the night of the dark moon is approaching, an elder or two from the *Oung* clan are selected and they keep watch, to determine the exact night of the dark moon. They sit there in the open, drinking their rice beer, watching the night skies. And then one morning, the elders would tuck a sprig of *Ngongnam* leaves behind their ears and seeing this, people come to know that in six days' time it will be the night of the dark moon. The role of the people is to start counting from the day they have sighted the elders wearing *Ngongnam* leaves, and prepare to herald in Naknyulum. At this time, whether he is married or not, a man will choose a girlfriend. He fashions a fine *kongkin*, a Jew's harp, as well as a fine-toothed comb, both made from bamboo, to present to his girlfriend when the time comes. All the girls stay up late stringing necklaces out of *kotshou* seeds, a non-edible variety of Job's tears. When the time comes, they also pound millet, and they make millet cakes as that will be their gift to their boyfriends.

On the night of the dark moon, that is the sixth day after the elders have sported the sprigs of *ngongnam*, the first rituals are performed. The next morning is the first day of Naknyulum. All the young men go into the forest to collect *lae*, green leaves to be used for wrapping the millet cakes, while the women collect firewood. Meanwhile, able-bodied men in the village slaughter pigs and a mithun or two. When the women come back with the firewood, they begin pounding the millet to make millet cakes, and the men cut up all the meat for cooking. In the evening, all the men take bunches of *ngongnam* leaves and dance up and down the village loudly chanting, "The light is coming!" And they tie these leaves at the door of their houses in all directions and even on the jutting peak of the roof in front. Some men tie the leaves on their field huts. This particular day is called S*ekka naknyet*, the first day.

On the second day, *Nakset*, nobody ventures out to the fields and the woods. Every one stays in the village, but they celebrate the festival by visiting relatives and offering portions of rice and meat to each other. All members of the village, young and old, brothers and sisters, gift each other food and strengthen their bonds. Cooked food wrapped in leaves is first offered to the elders of the *Oung* clan. The custom is that the young offer food to their elders and only after that, do the elders give them food. All the children congregate to play in the open, and the boys compete at games such as spinning wooden tops on the ground. In the evening, all the girls wrap a pack of four or five millet cakes *Jei wendek,* in a *lae* leaf, and in another leaf, they take a portion of *Naknyühsen* – the residue from the pot of rice brew. They then take these gifts to the houses of their boyfriends leaving them there with relatives of the boys. The boys in turn pass by the houses of the girls while they are on their way to the morung; the boys stop at the girls' houses and leave the Jew's harps and combs with the family members of the girls. In anticipation of this, the girls would have left the *Kotshou* seed-necklaces for the boys. All the boys sleep in the morung and go home the next morning.

The third day, *Sempounyet*, is spent by the men cleaning their *Hakhu*, or morungs; they spend the night playing the log drum every now and then until the light of a new day appears. At dawn they listen for the sounds of birds. If the first call they hear is the call of the *Aumeishou*, it is interpreted as the likelihood of sickness coming to the village; if it is the call of the *Mokpek*, it is good as it indicates success in hunting animals as well as heads; and if the first call heard is that of the *Aushoukaksak*, then it means that the enemy could vanquish them. Anyone who hears the first bird call starts to play the log drum. Following that, they eat up the millet cakes and the fermented rice brew that their girlfriends had left for them, and then they go home. Later in the day, the men clean and cut the paths along the way to the springs and the fields (but not the fields). The act of clearing the path is seen as an act of driving off all sickness and disease from the village.

On the fourth day, *Leibounyet,* nobody goes to the field lest they pollute the cleansing that was performed the day before. Instead, they spend the day either collecting firewood or wandering alongside the river.

It is believed that at the dawning of the fifth day, *Ngaobounyet,* all sickness has been driven away and the darkness is cast off, so everybody goes to the fields in the belief that if they work on this day, the harvest would be bountiful. The field work is done in a rotation system with groups formed in such a way that everybody takes a turn at working in each other's fields. It is referred to as *Nak-si-lüm*, or working the field to make the grains grow in abundance.

The next day, all the villagers go to the field where they have planted Job's tears. The labour of working the soil around the plants would have been completed in the previous month; only on the sixth day of the festival, *Lakpounyet*, do they clean the fields and loosen the soil around the plants. This is done in the belief that the Job's tears plants would grow healthy and become sweet to eat.

On the seventh day, *Nyetbou*, people go the field where they have planted *phemba*, cotton. They clear weeds and carefully clean the area around the plants. After their labours, they have a picnic feasting on the food they have brought from their homes.

On the eighth day, *Setbounyet*, nobody goes near their field for fear that if they did, their crops would fail. On the ninth and final day, known as *Gühbounyet*, people scrupulously avoid going to their fields. They believe that if they should violate this practice, a great wind will blow and bring heavy rains that would lash the crops; thunder and lightning would cause destruction for the crops and the people.

On these days, people relax and feast in the village, and in this celebratory mood, surrounded by friends and family, they bring the Naknyulum festival to a close.

This festival also marks the onset of winter and is also commemorated as the celebration of the new year. At this festival, there is no dancing, but the atmosphere is one of solemnity and prayerfulness because at this time, the creator, Shambulee, decides which soul should live and which soul should die in the coming year. The festival is like the Jewish New Year.

Different Chang villages use different names for the person who shot the tiger. The name Namumulou has been used here from the account told in Hakchang village, and some details from Tuensang Village are also included here. Unlike other festivals, there is no big community dancing during the Naknyulum festival; people emphasise the observation of traditions and rituals and prepare a feast and make merry amongst themselves.

Ngongnam leaves with their particular scent are stuffed into the nostril to stem nosebleeds.

Aumeishou: Rufus-Chinned Laughing Thrush

Mokpek: Owl

Aushoukaksak: Silver-eared Mesia

(Source: Folklore of Eastern Nagaland, Collected and Translated by Anungla Longkumer)

In addition, these are some other customs observed at Naknyulum:

During the period of the festival, outsiders and visitors are not allowed to enter the villages as they could be harmed by the spirits. The gate is closed for the duration of the festival and the people perform rituals to worship their creator-deity, Shambulee Muhgha, so that he might protect them from Usingkaklak, the devil. Changs believe that Shambulee Muhgha visits the houses late at night to receive the offerings of the people. On these visits, he also takes away the souls of those destined to die in that year. In their prayers, the people ask to be spared from death. The log drum is beaten to drive away Usingkaklak for he could come and steal the light. They also believe that the devil waits outside the gate to capture people, and this explains the strong taboo on people leaving the village in the festival period. The taboos of the festival are very severe; no engagements and marriages are allowed in this period.

The account of the darktime seems to have originated from the ancient enmity between Man and Tiger. Tiger sang a song that greatly angered Namumulo. Tiger's song went like this, 'I am going to eat you, I am going to hang your head around my neck like a necklace.' Man and Tiger could not possibly live together and they decided to have a contest. 'The one who is able to make fire first shall get to live in the village; and the loser must live in the woods.' Namu was the first man who made a fire. Tiger was sent into exile and he went to live in the forest. But he made attempts to kill women and children. In some accounts, the enmity between Man and Tiger is given as the reason for the dark time.

(Source: Chingmak Chang).

Acknowledgements

I am indebted to Chingmak Chang and the Chang community for graciously sharing insights into their culture, and for information on the festival of *Naknyulum* and names and words in the Chang language. The library of Tromsø for financial support and Barbican Press for believing in the book! Thank you all.